THE MARTLET BOX

THE MARTLET BOX

Jean Ross

CANONGATE · KELPIES

First published in 1987 by Canongate Publishing Ltd
First published by Canongate Kelpies in 1989

© 1987 by the estate of Jean Ross

Cover illustration by Alexa Rutherford

Printed and bound in Great Britain
by Cox and Wyman Ltd, Reading

ISBN 0 86241 280 3
CANONGATE PUBLISHING LTD
17 JEFFREY STREET, EDINBURGH EH1 1DR

to Susan and Anna

CHAPTER ONE

'The first time Uncle Henry saw the Captain,' Malcolm explained to his cousin Simon, 'was here, on this spot, in 1917.'

'No, no, no!' his great-uncle interrupted. 'It was further down the street.'

'Did you see his face?' Simon had lived in America for the last five years, and spoke with a faint transatlantic twang.

'Not clearly. He was wearing a black hat with a wide brim turned down. His collar was turned up, but in the faint light of the lamp I caught a glimpse of his eyes. That was enough.'

The boys shivered. It was a frosty evening a few days into January. Shadows in the narrow street seemed to nod in the fading light. Uncle Henry was pointing. 'All the buildings in the block — the ones I told you about, Malcolm — have been knocked down. Nothing left!'

'They'll be rebuilt,' Malcolm soothed him, peering through the palings at the raw, dead ground. Simon stared down the High Street. This was his first visit to Edinburgh and his Scottish relations. His father worked for a big oil company and before they had moved to the States the family had lived in France and Germany. He quite liked his cousin, though he found him a bit slow on the uptake, and was amazed by his great-uncle, who lived in a large Victorian house stuffed full of the relics of another age. But the City he loved, particularly the Old Town. He peered short-sightedly into the gathering shadows.

'Castlegate, Lawnmarket, High Street, Canongate,' he enum-
erated. 'From the air the High Street must look like a fish's
backbone, with all those little alleys leading off on either side.'

'We don't call them alleys in Edinburgh — they're called
wynds,' said Malcolm with a slight air of superiority. He liked
Simon well enough on short acquaintance but he felt slightly in
awe of him, although at thirteen he was slightly the elder of the
two. It was pleasant to be able to show off a little. After his father
had died a year ago in a car accident, Malcolm and his mother had
moved South, to London. He knew Edinburgh well, as a small
child had suffered nightmares about its sinister, winding streets.
He vividly remembered standing, clutching his mother's hand,
not far from this very spot. He had been about five at the time, and
a winter sunset had turned the evening sky to a threatening
crimson. It seemed to him that the tall chimneys of dockland Leith
had left their moorings and marched up the High Street towards
him, their smoke hair streaming. He had screamed in terror, and
refused to be comforted by his mother.

'Or closes, or vennels,' his great uncle was saying. 'Or if they've
got covered entrances they are called pends. They've been here
for hundreds of years. Many a bloody spulzie they must have
seen.'

'Spulzie?' queried Simon.

'A fight with drawn swords. Used to happen all the time. Two
men picking a fight over nothing and in a minute at each other's
throats. One of them left lying dead on the cobbles. Yes, it's seen
its fair share of murder, this city.' He sniffed about like an old dog
on the trail. 'Used to be a wynd just here,' he barked. 'Called
Henderson's. All gone now. Nothing but antique shops and
boutiques.' He spat the word out with contempt.

Malcolm, seeing that he was about to launch into a tirade on the
horrors of the modern age, tried to redirect his attention to the
past.

'But it was here that you and Grandma saw the Captain?'

'Of course. Haven't I told you? I was about your age.' He

shivered. A chill wind, salt from the Firth, seeped up the narrow street. The tall houses seemed to lean, whispering, above him.

'It's too cold to stand about. Let's go home and have some tea.'

***

When Ada his ancient housekeeper had brought in the tea tray there were toasted crumpets, dripping with butter, which Simon had never eaten before. Their great-uncle drew the heavy, shabby curtains against the dark and lit the gas fire. Under gentle pressure from Malcolm he resumed the story.

'It was just before Christmas. We had all gone up to town with our mother and Lucy's governess, Mouncie as we used to call her. We had tea at Patrick Thomson's and afterwards, as a great treat, we were allowed to go on our own to choose Christmas presents for the family. Children were more strictly brought up then, we felt it a bit of an adventure.'

'To go shopping? At *thirteen*?' Simon was incredulous.

'Yes, my lad. No films, well, not that we had seen, and no television in those days. We had to make up our own amusements. I remember Lucy, that's your grandmother, making . . .' Sensing another diversion, Malcolm moved swiftly in.

'Wasn't there a war on then?'

'Yes, of course, the Great War — the First World War. It didn't end until 1918. The streets were full of soldiers and sailors home on leave. That made it more exciting to us of course. Well, we hurried along the Bridges — I remember there were crowds of shoppers and we had to step off the pavement every so often with the jostling.

'There was noise all round, too, horses and drays rattling on the cobbled setts, trams, motors hooting, newsboys shouting. We were like swimmers breasting a choppy sea, holding hands to keep together. We knew exactly where we were going; a little curio shop in the High Street where Lucy had seen a brooch she wanted to give to Mother, and I was after a pearl-handled penknife. So we made our way towards the corner of the Bridges and High Street, opposite the Tron Kirk.

9

'We reached it, breathless. We began to walk briskly down the narrow High Street, for we had promised to be back "not a minute after a quarter past five". Then Lucy stopped still, and I fell against her and we both stood silent.

'The silence was like a — a kind of singing in our ears, but it wasn't that. What we both saw and felt now was different. It was alien. *It was not the High Street we knew*. At least it was and it wasn't. First there were the houses. In my childhood, before all this dolling up and restoration, they were a deal more ruinous, but now they seemed to have changed out of all recognition. They towered above us — seven, eight storeys high, with overhanging wooden fronts and hooded windows. The only lighting in the street came from those windows and from lanterns suspended in archways or at the mouths of the wynds. And gradually, as though it had been there all the time and was only then seeping into our consciousness, we became aware of a teeming life in those alleys, in the street itself, a rushing, bustling, yet at first soundless hurry all about us.

'Women, shawled and hurrying or in wide skirts which they lifted disdainfully over the rubbish which lay all around. Men cloaked, with tricorn hats, boys barefoot in ragged breeches, horses, cows, pigs, even chickens — all hastening up and down the street. And finally, as though we had been in the process of tuning in to it, there came to our ears a mixed medley: music, shouts, horses' hooves, drunken singing, street cries. And the smell — I can't even describe it! Suddenly, we were frightened. We turned to run back the way we had come. And then we saw him.

'He was standing in the light of one of those overhead lanterns, so that his head and shoulders were silhouetted. He was turned slightly away from us, looking up-street towards the Tron. There was something, even then, which so disturbed me — some indefinable quality of menace in his quietly waiting there — that I froze, and Lucy with me. I pulled her back into the shadows. As we watched, he half turned his head in our direction. That was the first time I saw his face. It was an unhealthy colour, like clay, with eyes so deep set that in the shadow of his hat you couldn't make them out, just dark hollows.

'We did not dare breathe until he turned away. Then we ran. Down the nearest close to our left we flew, not stopping until we saw it had widened into a courtyard, a dead end.'

Uncle Henry paused. His hands covered his face.

'I can see that court now! I could not have imagined it! It was quite brightly lit, from windows above street level. We could hear music and laughter coming from one towered chamber. All we wanted, though, was somewhere to hide as quickly as possible. So we ran towards a corner were a dim light shone from the rounded window of a little shop.

'The door stood slightly open, and was up a flight of about half a dozen steps, so that the window was above our eye level. We climbed the steps the better to see in. An Aladdin's cave met our eyes; such a press of objects all jumbled together that it would be difficult to recall all that was there.

'I can't remember if it was Lucy or I who took the courage to open the door and venture into the shop. I do remember it was lit by a lantern which swung above our heads from a beam and in this wavering light we made out a room piled to the ceiling with treasures — a shining tumble of baubles, buckles, brooches, bundles of spoons, tall Chinese vases, candlesticks, chairs, silk gowns, snuff boxes, parasols, shoes, suits of rusty armour and, hangling like stalactites from the shadows above, a tawdry swing of silk handkershiefs and cravats. Immediately facing us was a long table, which appeared to serve as some kind of shop counter, for in the midst of a pile of brooches, necklaces and rings, glittering, it seemed to us, with precious stones, was a notice which announced in a flowing hand:

Orra Things Bought and Sold

I was reading this and wondering what it meant, while Lucy

picked over a pewter plateful of trinkets, when we became aware of an old man staring at us over the table.

'I don't know whether the shopkeeper, for it was he, had come in unobserved by us, or whether he had been there in the shadows all the time. He was as curious to look at as his wares. His eyes behind steel-rimmed spectacles were at once pale and piercing; he was clean shaven but had a wart at one side of his chin. His straggling white hair fell down over the collar of a coat the colour of standing tea and he had a dirty piece of linen, knotted cravat-like, round his neck. He leaned eagerly forward, peering at Lucy and it became immediately apparent that he was disappointed. Whoever he had been expecting, it was certainly not us.

'From that moment on, he could not wait to get rid of us. Whether we bought anything or not didn't matter. He muttered under his breath in a thick, indistinct dialect, shuffled repeatedly to the window and back, urged us to make haste, as it was time to put up the shutters. But Lucy was not to be hurried — you know your grandmother, Malcolm. Also, it seems strange now, but we were quite enjoying ourselves. We had forgotten about the sinister figure under the lamp-post, forgotten that we seemed to have slipped back in time at least a hundred and fifty years. It was a real adventure at last. Lucy was examining a silver brooch; I had discovered a little paper knife with an ornamental handle, when the old man, coming up close to us, at last seemed to notice something odd in our dress or conversation. He looked at us strangely, shaking his head. Then he asked, with a sort of sideways cunning glance: "And what year — what year will you be at then?". Before I could speak, Lucy answered, "Nineteen Seventeen". At this he seemed to make up his mind. Cramming into our hands the little brooch and the knife, he pushed us before him into the darkness at the back of the room.

'He hurpled over to the window once again, and what he saw from there seemed to have given him a nasty shock, for he hurriedly reached the lantern down from its hook and unlocked a door which we had not seen before, half-hidden as it was behind a dusty velvet curtain. Through this door he bundled us, into a dark, narrow passage which smelled strongly of cabbage. As it swung to behind us, we heard the unmistakable sounds of heavy knocking on the shop door, which the shopkeeper had bolted and barred only minutes before.

'Holding the lantern up, he scrutinised us. His eyes were frightened, and they peered deep into ours with a desperate intensity, as though he would read our very souls.

'"So, so, so,"' he muttered. "So that's the way of it. These are the ones who are found worthy, eh?" all of which made no sense to us.

'He shuffled on down the narrow, evil-smelling passage. Behind us, we could hear very clearly now the thump, thump of someone beating on the outer door with a heavy object. Somehow, neither of us needed to ask who this might be.

'At the end of the passage he bent down and placed the lantern on the floor, which was bare boards, rather worm-eaten. At this point there were some steps downwards, stone flagged, and it was one of these flags that he lifted, with much groaning. I thought that perhaps he was going to reveal a secret passageway, but there was nothing but a shallow cavity below. Out of it he took an oblong packet which appeared to be wrapped in several thicknesses of woollen cloth. It was about eight inches long by five wide.

'"*Deliver this to Mistress Clarke, and into no hands else,*" he ordered, pressing it on me. "And now hurry, for the Lord's sake hurry. Follow the steps down and ye'll find a door . . ." He was already making his way back to the shop.

'"*What* Mistress Clarke?" Lucy demanded. But he was already out of hearing. "She'll make herself known," I thought I heard him say — Lucy heard nothing. We hurried down the stairs. There was, indeed, a door at the bottom. We pushed at it and it opened easily. Lucy hung back.

'"Come *on*!" I hissed at her. "Don't you know who that is knocking? D'you want him to nab you too?" She was bending down, replacing the loose stone and laying something upon it.

"I've paid for the brooch and the knife" she said primly. Then we were out into the street. I pulled the door shut behind me.

'A car chugged past us, going downhill; the snell, fresh wind blowing through snow, came to meet us from the Forth. We turned left, and ran up the High Street, which was now just as we had always known it — dim wartime blue lighting, people, motors, horses and carts. Lucy stopped and showed me the shopping bag she was still carrying. "Put *that* in there" she ordered. "I've put in the brooch and the knife. We don't want to have to answer any questions. We're late enough as it is." When we got home Mother was furious. We were given a wigging and told we would have bread and milk for our suppers. It was another world then.'

Uncle Henry sighed, and paused to light a small cigar.

'When you got home, what did you do with the parcel?' Simon asked. His thin, spectacled face was expressionless, his voice polite. Malcolm leaned forward, tea forgotten. He had heard the story more than once before, still he was spellbound by it.

'We did nothing immediately,' replied their uncle. 'There was all this stramash when we got back — the usual sort of fuss that always attended my mother's arrival. Father had to be called and told of our naughtiness (and to add his scoldings to hers), bags had to be unloaded, parcels unwrapped . . .'

'But what about *your* parcel?'

'Oh yes. Well, it was still in Lucy's shopping bag, and when Mouncie tried to snatch it from her your grandmother was more than a match for her!

'"Oh no," she told her sweetly. "Our secret Christmas presents are in that, and they mustn't be seen until Christmas morning, you know."

'Mouncie was a stupid woman, good-hearted, but slow and sentimental. She accepted it without question.'

'And where did you put it?'

'At first in Lucy's bedroom. But it couldn't be left there, because nothing was safe from mother and the maids. So Lucy had the brilliant idea of rewrapping it, labelling it *"Christmas present — not to be opened"*, and putting it on the top of the shelf of the bookcase in the schoolroom. So that's what she did, before we had to go and wash our hands for supper.'

'Bread and milk.' Malcolm made a face.

'Actually it was hot milk and Abernethy biscuits. Anyway, as soon as we'd undressed and got rid of Mouncie, Lucy crept up into my room. That's the one we use as the spare room now — the one you boys are in. She had hidden the two gifts in her handkerchief, so we opened the bedroom door and, by the light of the landing gaslight, we examined them.

'That was when we got our first shock. A rusty ornament which might have been anything, and a knife, black with the dirt of ages, the blade worn away to a thin red worm of rust. Lucy was furious. "What a rotten swizz!" she said. "I put down five shillings for those, and look at them!" (That was quite a lot of money in those days — more like five or even ten pounds now. We'd been saving our pocket money for weeks.) "I'm going right back there tomorrow," she continued. "I'll jolly well tell him what I think of him."

'I just looked at her. Then I reminded her that neither the brooch nor the knife had been like that when we took them. And I pointed to the stone in the midst of the rusty metal. I was sure it was an amethyst, I told her, and the knife handle was silver and mother of pearl. But nothing I could say would console her. She just went on and on about how she had been cheated, and how she was going to go back there and demand her money back.

'"Well, you won't find him or his shop," I said when I could get a word in edgeways. That brought her to a standstill. Up to that minute we had been so occupied with being late, and being punished and hiding the parcel, that we had refused to think about what had actually *happened* that afternoon. We hadn't even discussed it.

'Anyway, Lucy was not going to admit now that anything out of the way had occurred. She'd been frightened, yes, but now she was determined to find a rational explanation. (You're very like your grandma in that, Simon.) So she said that these weren't the same things that we had bought in the shop — the old man had palmed this rubbish off on us at the last moment, by some sleight of hand. There was no point in arguing with her, so I agreed to go with her to ask for a refund, and sent her off to her own room.

'When she had gone I took the brooch down to the bathroom and scrubbed some of the dirt off, and although the metal was still black you could see it had been finely engraved. And the central stone, as large as a five pence piece, came up shining like a violet after rain — it *was* an amethyst, and a beauty. Later on I begged some metal polish off the housemaid and went at it with an old toothbrush. It came up quite well in the end. Lucy kept it for herself, because too many questions would have been asked had we given it to our mother. I think she's lost it by now.'

'Did Gran ever admit she was wrong — about the brooch, I mean?' Simon asked.

'Your grandmother isn't good at apologising,' Uncle Henry said wryly. The boys remembered that the two were not supposed to be on good terms nowadays.

'And what about the mysterious package?'

There was a knock at the door which made Malcolm jump, and Ada poked her head round.

'If you're finished with the tea things I'll clear away now, Mr Gilchrist.' She clattered cups onto a tray. 'What would you be wanting for your dinner? There's thae pork chops need eating up before they go off, or a nice bit of smoked fish.' She did not ask the boys what they would like, nor did she approve of them having dinner with their uncle as if they were grown up.

'Anything — anything at all, Ada,' Uncle Henry replied. 'As long as it's not hot milk and biscuits.' He seemed to think he had made a good joke.

CHAPTER TWO

A fter dinner they returned to the study. Malcolm, large for his age, with fair, floppy hair and a round, cheerful face, sprawled in one of the shabby leather-covered armchairs, while his great-uncle made himself comfortable in his great wing-backed chair. Simon lay on the hearthrug, his head propped on a cushion. His eyes were closed behind his glasses.

They drank their coffee.

'Did you go back to the High Street the next day, then?'

'No, not the next day, the following Saturday. Lucy developed a bad cold. She was a delicate girl, that's why she had a governess and didn't go to school. I had just started at Watson's. Yes, the following Saturday, in the morning, I got permission to go on condition I went straight to the shop and came straight back home again. I had said I still had a couple of presents to get, which was the truth really. It was bitterly cold, I remember, and snowing a little. Thin, thready flakes blowing along the iron hard ground. I walked up the Mound, and hurried to the High Street (I had told Mother that I was going back to the curio shop we were originally making for). It all looked so different in daylight. Grubby and dilapidated, but nothing sinister about it! Just tenements, falling into disrepair.

'I walked fast down to the Tron Kirk, crossed over the Bridges. Then I thought to myself — now, go slow — it must be one of the turnings past Niddry Street. When I came to Blackfriars Street it seemed to me that this must be the road we came out in. But I couldn't find the courtyard with the shop. I went back, thinking I

17

must have missed it. There *was* a wynd, much nearer the Bridges, but it went down, narrow all the way. There was no other opening between that and Niddry Street. So, back I went to Blackfriars Street.'

'Looking for the door you came out of?'

Uncle Henry nodded. 'And I found it!'

Simon sat up. 'You found the door?'

'The very door!'

'How did you know it was the one?'

'First, it was exactly where it should have been. But when I tried to open it it wouldn't budge. It was stuck — just a little ajar. So I looked up and down the street, to see that nobody was looking — and I set my shoulder to it, and forced it open.'

'Well?'

'It gave onto a ruin, open to the sky. There were a few steps going up, and then all beyond was blocked by a fall of rubble. But, on the topmost step, in the thin mantle of snow, something glittered. I looked closer. There were two new half-crowns.'

Uncle Henry paused, but neither boy spoke.

'And the step beneath was loose. I was able to prise it up quite easily. There was a hollow beneath it, just large enough to take a package the size of a double tea-caddy, wrapped in two thicknesses of cloth. And in the corner of the hole was a wisp of that coarse, hairy wool, a few threads, no more. I pocketed that and the money, to show Lucy. A woman saw me creeping out of the door and made as if to speak to me, but I strolled off as nonchalantly as possible, whistling.

'Then I went to the curio shop in the High Street, the one we had been aiming for when our adventure overtook us. I bought a little gilt box for stamps for Mother, a paperweight for Father, and a penknife with a mother of pearl handle for Lucy to give Mother. I asked the woman in there how long the buildings opposite had been ruins, and she told me they'd been empty for years, and had gradually fallen down. When I mentioned something about a courtyard it meant nothing to her.'

Simon nodded slowly. 'So I guess, uncle, you feel you and Gran had been doing a bit of time-travelling, like those two women who went to Versailles and found themselves back in the time of the French Revolution — saw Marie Antoinette sketching — saw the Guards running and so on.'*

'I know the story you mean,' agreed Uncle Henry. 'Some people called it mass hallucination; but it was well authenticated. The uniforms were all correct for one thing, and the plan of the gardens. Those two women could never have known such details.'

'And did you tell Gran all this?'

'Yes, but it made no difference. And, shortly afterwards, first she and then I went down with measles. It spoiled Christmas completely — I had it quite badly — it affected my eyesight. So, what with one thing and another, the business of the package was — not exactly forgotten, but pushed into the background to be dealt with later.'

'And it was left on the shelf, in full view?'

'No, Lucy had had the sense to hide it behind the old Chambers Encyclopaedia. Father had just bought a complete new set of the Encyclopaedia Britannica, so it wasn't likely anyone would start looking at the old lot.'

There was a lengthy silence.

'But did you really imagine —' Simon hesitated, he had to be tactful, 'that some day this Mistress Clarke would knock on the door, or perhaps, bearing in mind that she must have been dead for well over a hundred years, appear in ghostly form, and say, "Prithee, I am Mistress Clarke and I demand that you hand me straightway yonder package!"' He laughed. His great-uncle did not.

'I told you before, I was pretty ill. I had to lie in a darkened room because of my eyes, and I felt miserable. I was far more sorry for myself at that time than I was curious about what was going to happen to the package — or even what was inside it. That came later, when I was convalescing.'

* *An Adventure*, by Miss Moberley and Miss Jourdain, published 1911.

The boys watched him, knowing that he did not see the room in which they were sitting, with its knee-hole desk, comfortable armchairs and soft lighting, but a different sixty-year memory; the schoolroom with its round table, ink-stained cloth, flaring gas globes, sulky fire — and a bookcase full of geography, history, French and Latin textbooks, rising to the old encyclopaedias on the top shelf.

'It was one afternoon, well into January, that I was sitting with Lucy in the schoolroom, not well enough to go back to Watson's, and bored with not having enough to do, that we brought up the subject. At least, Lucy did. I can see her now, in her pinafore, sitting on the other side of the fire, her head bent over a book. Suddenly she looked up, folded her arms. "Well," she said, "are you going to just let it stay up there?"

'"What are you talking about?" I asked innocently.

'"That parcel," says she. "Are you going to let it moulder there forever, without trying to find out what's in it?"

'I was flabbergasted. "We promised," I stuttered, "We gave our word. Nobody but Mistress Clarke."

'"So you still think she'll be coming along?" Lucy sneered. "You really believe all that tommy-rot?"

'"Not exactly, but —"

'"Well then, *Master* Harry!" Lucy rose and crossed over to me, bending down to peer into my face. "I dare you! I dare you to get onto that chair — you're taller than me — and fetch it down right this minute. Then we'll open it and see what's in it, once and for all!"

'"Someone might come in . . ."

'"Nonsense. Mouncie's out, as you well know, Mother's having tea with Lady Tullich and Father won't be home for at least an hour. Anyway, what if they do? What do you expect to find in it — a tarantula spider? It's probably empty."

'I couldn't explain to her without sounding silly that I just felt it was wrong; we'd given our word. She just kept on and on at me.

'"Don't be such a gowk," she said. "Are you frightened it might bring *him* after you?"

'"The man under the lamp?" I whispered. "We haven't been so lucky, you know."

'"You mean the measles — and your eyes? You're crackers! All you're doing my lad, is wasting time. There may never be another opportunity like this. Get on that chair — well, if you won't, I will!"

'My hands round the book I was holding were so damp with sweat the red dye came off on my fingers. Of course she was right. I *was* scared of that abominable box. I felt it was like Pandora's Box in the legends. Once we'd opened it we should be sorry. And then it would be too late.

'I heard her dragging a chair over to the bookshelf, looked up to see her perched on it, stretching up to the highest shelf. I half-hoped she wouldn't be able to reach it, but she was moving the books. From the back of the shelf she drew out the parcel. "Feech!" she coughed and sneezed. "It's filthy dirty. Here, you take it. I feel peculiar — all that stretching's made me giddy!"

'She did sound odd, quite unlike herself for a moment. "Henry!" she called again, almost pleading. When she called me Henry like that, I knew she meant what she said. At last I went to help her.

'We put the parcel on the hearth. We undid the paper, then came to the woollen wrappings. They were black with age, in places metal showed through. We used the schoolroom scissors to cut them away, then burned them. In the fire they just melted away, burning brightly with a gassy blue flame for a moment. Lucy went to wash her hands and came back saying, "There, that's better!"

'Then we looked at the box.

'For that was what the parcel contained. A metal box, a casket, black with dirt and time. Hard to say what kind of metal. The lid was arched, the sides ornamented with a curious frieze of birds and flowers. There was a keyhole, but no key. We argued as to whether we should force it open — but did not know how. I did not even want to touch it.

21

'Lucy turned the little coffer this way and that. She began to shake it, to see if it rattled. Just at that moment we heard footsteps, and a door closing. In the hall we heard Mamma's voice, talking to Morris the tablemaid. Quick as a wink, Lucy slipped the box under the table, where it was hidden by the long chenille cloth. Mamma came in, still wearing her hat.

'"My dears," she said, "whatever have you been doing? Burning something? There's a horrid smell and the fire's quite choked."

'Lucy muttered something about burning some old painting cloths, and Mamma called Morris to see to the fire. Then we were shooed off to tidy ourselves up for supper, so it was not until later that evening, when the grown-ups were all downstairs at dinner, that we could look at the box again. When we were supposed to be in bed, Lucy, who had slipped into the schoolroom and removed it from its temporary hiding place, brought it to my room.'

'How did you open it?' Simon wanted to know. 'With a knife?'

'No, no.' Their uncle spoke slowly, as though reluctant. 'I — I was turning it about in my hands, thinking how light it was, that there *couldn't* be anything in it, and my fingers touched a secret spring, worked by the centre of a flower. The lid sprang open. I had a strange feeling that if it had not been meant that I should open it at that moment, I might have pressed all the flowers, or leaves, or strange swallow-like birds which decorated the little casket, and it would not have opened to me or anyone.'

There was a pause.

'And?' Simon spoke softly.

'There was very little inside. It was lined with a soft green material, like velvet. And in the midst of this was a — a small round thing, which looked at first like a roll of gauze, wound tight, and about the size of a golf ball. No colour to it. I felt a strange reluctance to touch it. It fascinated and repelled me at the same time. But Lucy had no such inhibitions. She put her fingers into the box to take hold of it — and then she gave a little shriek! She drew back, and made me try. It was the oddest feeling — like touching sticky cobwebs which melt and form again when you take your hand away. My fingers went *through* it. You couldn't lift it. Then Lucy said, "I wish I could think how to get it out," with an absolutely concentrated, determined look on her face. The little ball just rose into the air, light as thistledown, and floated down onto my eiderdown, swaying a little in the draught.'

'It was the draught, then,' Simon said.

'Yes, from the open door. But the little ball wasn't in the draught *inside* the box.' Uncle Henry sounded tetchy. He resumed his story.

'We looked at one another. We didn't dare touch it again. Lucy was shivering, I remember — very cold those bedrooms were then — no fires. She had wrapped her eiderdown round her. "You blew it," I accused her.

'"No I didn't — cross my heart," she kept saying. "I just wished it out of the box. That's all." I could tell it had shaken her.

'"Don't be daft," I told her. I kept my eyes fixed on the little ball. It was trembling and glistening like a blob of soap suds. I was afraid that, like a bubble, it would pop into a patch of damp. I imagined it was getting smaller, so I said, "Well, I wish it had never got out of that box, for Lord knows how we're going to get it back in again; we might be up all night."

'"So much for your wishing," Lucy said, "How hard did you wish?"

'"I didn't wish hard," I told her, "I just said it."

'"Well, watch this!" Lucy said. "I think I have the hang of it!" She stood with her body tensed above the thing and hissed in a low voice: "I *will* that this little ball go back into the box."

'At once the ball whisked into the air, floated a foot or so to the right, and came down plump — right in the centre of the piece of dusty velvet inside the casket.

'Well, after that, of course, I wanted a go at it. I willed it out of the box onto the dressing-table. But I wasn't good at it, like Lucy. Perhaps it was to do with being ill, weak and excited. Anyway it was a terrible effort to hold the thought. It kept wavering and changing direction and I broke out into a sweat. In the end Lucy

23

held my hand. I felt strength like a warm current coming from her to me — and the ball lifted as easy as a feather, and came to rest before the mirror.

'I lay back on the pillows, quite giddy. So Lucy had to will it back again into the box, and said that that was quite enough for one evening. She asked me if I could remember which flower I had pressed to open it — that was easy, it was slightly larger than the others, and then she shut it with a snap. For a moment I rather wished that it might stay shut forever, but when she made me try, the lid flew open as easy as it had the first time.

'She took it back to her room, and hid it under the roof of her dolls' house, which lifted off. After that, we'd sneak off and play with it whenever we had the opportunity. Usually after we went to bed. We got quite clever at moving the ball; it took less effort each time, but you had to concentrate. The moment you thought of something else it wavered or fell to the floor. One day it disappeared completely, in mid-air. That gave us a nasty fright. We had to will it, both together, to return, and it took a long time coming.

'And then we found out that, in the middle of willing the ball to go to the top of the wardrobe, Lucy suddenly wondered whether she'd left the tap running in the bathroom — all her thoughts were there, so we knew that was where it must have gone. That put us in an awful tizzy. Suppose she'd thought of the top of Arthur's Seat, or the Eiffel Tower, or the Taj Mahal, or even the dining-room downstairs, where Father and Mother were entertaining Dr and Mrs Foggie to dinner. It was too awful to contemplate.'

'I would have thought of that possibility almost at once,' Simon told his uncle, in an irritatingly superior voice.

'I shouldn't,' Malcolm said, adding, "but I wouldn't have kept on doing the same experiments over and over again. Couldn't you have changed its shape or something?'

'Yes, yes, we come to that later.' Uncle Henry brushed him aside. 'One thing at a time.'

Simon sighed. 'So you sent the ball travelling?'

'Safe places at first, like the housemaid's pantry. One of us would go there, see it arrive, and wait to waft it back. We had some narrow squeaks. Once Mouncie caught me, in my dressing-gown, downstairs in the drawing-room. She thought I'd sneaked down to help myself to chocolates. I said I'd left a book behind. Fortunately we'd just sent the ball upstairs.

'Then we got bolder. I went halfway up King Arthur's Seat and Lucy sent me the ball. I can still remember the thrill of that moment. Timing it on my new watch, and then seeing it materialise out of nowhere and float down on the turf beside me. Right on time. We'd found out, you see, that if we didn't imagine it travelling, but only saw it arriving, it would get there instantly. Anyway, just as I was about to send it back, a gang of keelies, rough kind of boys, were on me, nearly knocking me senseless. They had a feud with the Watson's boys. I offered little resistance — there was no point. Fortunately a park-keeper appeared and they made off, leaving me with a bloody nose. I wiped my face as best I could — and then remembered the ball! I hoped that Lucy had recovered it as I couldn't find it anywhere — and thank heavens, she had. I got a thrashing from Father when I returned home, for being in a brawl, and was forbidden to go out again on my own until I returned to school.'

'And then?'

'Time you were in bed, boys, it's well after ten. You can tell Simon the tale upstairs. I'm tired of talking. So long ago, and such a waste. A waste of time, and energy, and hope.'

Simon looked at Malcolm, who shook his head.

They said their goodnights and went upstairs.

CHAPTER THREE

L ater that night, in that same room which in their great-uncle's
day had been cold, gaslit and cheerless, and which now had
twin divans, bedside lights and central heating, the boys lay in bed
talking.

'Why did the old boy stop there?' enquired Simon.

'Because — oh, because he doesn't come out too well in the
next bit of the story.'

Simon switched off his lamp. He leaned back, clasping his
hands behind his head.

'You believe it all?'

'Mm-phm.'

'Bit far-fetched, isn't it?'

'Not if you know the facts.'

Simon yawned. 'Thought you said they never did — know
everything, I mean.' There was silence for a while. Then Malcolm
said, solemnly: 'You can measure thought-waves, you know.'

'Oh yes? where did you read that tit-bit, in the *Psychic Journal* or
the *Reader's Digest*?'

'Actually,' Malcolm retorted with dignity, 'it was on the science
page of the *Guardian*. Apparently it's like radio waves but
stronger. You measure it with an encephalograph.' He stumbled
slightly over the word.

'So you're suggesting that Gran and Uncle Harry were
whizzing this Fairy Liquid golf ball about by exercising their
powers of thought? Incidentally what scientific theory do you have

for the ball itself — perhaps a flying saucer left it behind on a day trip, or . . .'

'If you're going to treat everything in that way,' Malcolm interrupted him, 'then there's no point in continuing this discussion.' He thumped his pillow rather ostentatiously and lay down, pulling the blankets up almost over his head.

Simon felt rather guilty; he was fond of his cousin, regarding him rather as Dr Watson to his Sherlock Holmes. He attempted reconciliation.

'I'm sorry, Mal, it's just that it all seems so fantastic, and you know I'm one of those people that can't take a story without facts to back it up. Very dull and plodding, I know. I wish I had your imagination.'

Needled, Malcolm stuck his head out of the bedclothes again.

'It's *not* just imagination — there are plenty of hard facts if you'd just listen to the whole story. And if you really want to know, yes I do have an explanation for the ball — I think it was a sort of — of essence of matter.' This last came out in a bit of a rush.

Simon trod carefully.

'Essence of matter — hmm, do you mean atoms, molecules, DNA, that sort of thing?'

'Sort of,' Malcolm said. He knew Simon was supposed to be clever at science and he was afraid of making a fool of himself. 'You know how nothing is really solid — that we and all the objects around us are made up of trillions of tiny particles, all going at different speeds, although to the naked eye they look solid enough — even feel pretty solid if you bump into them. Well, suppose we — or an object like the ball — were going thousands of times faster. We'd be able to pass through apparently solid pieces of furniture, even disappear altogether.'

Simon was silent for a while. He was quite surprised that his cousin seemed to be taking this whole story so seriously, and was tempted to make another sarcastic remark about scientific theory, but he wisely held his tongue.

'So you think that this piece of gauzy material inside the casket was in fact a hitherto undiscovered manifestation of a type of — let's call it matter — which could be manipulated by the power of thought-waves through space?' he enquired, keeping his voice neutral. 'That's certainly a very interesting idea. What else could they do with it — change it into something different?'

'Yes, as a matter of fact they —' Malcolm broke off. 'I don't think you *really* believe me,' he said accusingly. 'I think you ought to hear the rest of the story from Uncle Henry. *If* he can be persuaded to tell it. I'm going to sleep now.'

This time, Simon could tell, Malcolm really was not going to be coerced into saying any more. He was soon breathing regularly and deeply, apparently fast asleep. Simon lay awake for some time. He was intrigued by the story, not because he believed any part of it, but because he was fascinated by psychology. He considered his great-uncle to be perfect material for a case history, and fully intended to question him again in the morning.

Uncle Henry did not appear until the boys had almost finished their breakfast. He looked as if he had not slept, his thin hair was ruffled, his eyes dim as a fish that has lain too long on the slab.

He was not talkative, and soon disappeared behind his copy of *The Scotsman*. Simon attempted conversation.

'There's been a hard frost,' he remarked. 'It looks as if it might snow. Perhaps we should try out that pair of old skates we saw in the attic the other day — remember, Mal?'

He was not a good skater, in spite of New England winters, but he wished to provoke his uncle, who peered at him over the top of the paper.

'I very much doubt if there's been enough frost yet. You could go up to Craiglockhart and see but I doubt if the ice will be bearing. They won't let you on if it isn't. Winters are not what they were.'

'Was it a hard winter? The one you were telling us about in 1917?'

'Very hard indeed,' Uncle Henry replied dismissively.

28

Simon was about to reopen the questioning when Ada bustled in, a shrivelled, monkey-like old woman in a green nylon overall.

'Yon Bina was round asking for you, Malcolm,' she announced in her harsh voice.

'Who's Bina?' Simon asked.

'Oh, just a girl. She's not bad, lives next door. Goes to Gillespie's High,' Malcolm replied nonchalantly.

'If you're going to skate,' their uncle said testily, 'you'd better get on with it and not sit around gossiping like a pair of old women.' He bit viciously into a piece of toast. He was definitely not in a good mood, and the boys decided to keep out of his way for a while. Malcolm led the way to the attic. It was surprisingly large, divided into two rooms, and cluttered with boxes, trunks and old newspapers. Two skylights, one to each room, provided light.

The skates, when unearthed, proved to be so rusty and old-fashioned that even if they had fitted either of the boys, they would have been rejected. On the skylights, the first soft flakes of snow had started to settle. Simon had discovered a cardboard box full of old 78 rpm gramophone records, and an ancient, though not antique, wind-up player. The tinny sound of long-forgotten pre-war dance bands scratched and thumped through a medley of once-popular tunes.

Malcolm had uncovered a boxful of old photographs, some in tarnished frames. One he held out to Simon showed a stiffly posed girl and boy of about their own age. The girl sat smugly smirking, her long hair gathered back into a big bow at the nape of her neck. She wore a pleated skirt, a sailor blouse, and had her ankles neatly crossed. By her side stood a boy in a kilt, one hand on the back of her chair. He was not unlike Malcolm, but fairer. His round face, with a puzzled look, gazed out at them, as though he had asked a question but got no answer.

'Grandma and *him*?'

Nodding, Malcolm replaced the picture in its box. The record scratched to an end and they became aware of their uncle's voice calling them, presumably from the landing door below. Feeling rather guilty, though for what reason they were not sure, they clattered down the uncarpeted stairs. He was waiting on the landing, looking out of the window. The snow was falling quite thickly now.

'I came to tell you that I am going out for a while and I doubt if I'll be back for lunch. I have to go to my bank and since my club is near there I have arranged to meet an old friend there at one o'clock.'

There was an awkward silence. The boys wondered what to say.

'So you'll have to amuse yourselves — I doubt if I'll be back much before teatime. Perhaps if you rang your grandmother she might have you over. It's quite an easy journey . . .' His voice faded, and he cleared his throat.

'I must — apologise for my bad temper this morning. Not really used to having boys of your age around, not that I don't enjoy it of course. Forgive an old man's grumpiness. I wondered . . .' Another long pause. 'I wondered if you would like to read this.'

His hand shot out from behind his back, bearing a rather grubby red exercise book, of the kind sold in Woolworth's. Simon took it, opening it to the first page.

'No, no — don't read it now,' their uncle said hastily. 'I'm afraid I couldn't finish the — tale — I was telling you last night. I find it rather distressing — at any rate I remembered that some years ago I wrote it down. Thought it might make a good fairy story.' He laughed humourlessly and turned away. The boys watched him shuffle off down the corridor.

'It's pointless us *both* trying to read this,' Malcolm complained some minutes later, attempting to decipher Uncle Henry's spidery hand.

'Let me read it — I know his writing.'

Simon lay back on the rug, watching through the window as the snow fell thick and steady against a sky the colour of dirty aluminium. Malcolm's voice droned a little to start with, then strengthened and took on colour as the story unfolded.

30

'It must have been early February,' wrote Uncle Henry, 'when we got our first real breakthrough. Just before I went back to school. Father had set me some work to do, geometry — something to do with a pentagram. The five-sided figure was in my mind, and Lucy, who was a bit bored with it all, was sitting opposite me with the ball resting on a handkerchief in her lap. I was drawing in my exercise book, in red ink. And suddenly, the ball wasn't a ball any longer, but a starfish, with five tentacles!

'I got such a fright that I let out a shout. Lucy had just time to see it before it was back in its ball shape. Of course, we had to talk it over and try it again — and again it happened! It was better this time. We suddenly got very excited, because we realised that we had in our hands something that could be moulded into — well, the possibilities were endless.

'We had to begin at the beginning, though. It was far harder than moving the ball. Just as Lucy had managed that better than I, so now I found that I was better at creating than she was. She simply couldn't imagine things — couldn't concentrate on them. We made some glorious mistakes between us! Pen holders like snakes, cups like mushrooms, a pin-cushion like a cabbage — a daisy like something out of a child's drawing book. It really is very difficult to imagine how something even as commonplace as a daisy looks when you don't have it in front of you. Anyway, as we got better at it, we got more and more ambitious, and heaven knows what might have happened if something hadn't occurred that put a stop to all our experiments.'

CHAPTER FOUR

'It was early March before I was finally back at school, and I had missed so many lessons that I had to have extra tuition, which meant I often didn't get home until half-past five. One evening, at about this time, I came home to find Lucy waiting for me in the hall. I remember I was freezing cold — it had been snowing again — and wanted to make straight for a fire, but Lucy dragged me into the downstairs cloakroom. She was in a state of great excitement.

'"Something's happened," she hissed. She was stuttering, most unusual for her. Bit by bit, however, out it all came. It was Mother's Red Cross Committee afternoon, and an important one, for the Commissioner was expected. Every Monday all those ladies sat up in our drawing-room rolling bandages and making little pads filled with sphagnum moss for dressings — and feeling they were really helping the war effort in a big way. Then Mother would give them tea and cakes, and once in a while they had a speaker to address them. Today was one of those occasions — someone to give them a little pep talk. But today it was someone special.

'"You'll never guess who," spluttered Lucy.

'"Well, get on with it and tell me," I said, for I was tired and cold and my head was full of algebra.

'"A real live spy from British Intelligence!" she brought out triumphantly.

'"Don't be daft," I said. "If he was really a spy he wouldn't come here talking about it!"

'"It's not a he, it's a she. And of course she didn't announce it. But it's obvious from the stories she was telling. All before the war of course, but absolutely thrilling — in the Balkans, in Russia and Turkey, even in Mongolia! I just *know* she's a spy. Anyway — that's not the most important thing. Guess what her name is? *Mrs Clarke!*"

'"Mrs Clarke?" I echoed stupidly.

'"*Mistress Clarke* then." Lucy clutched my arm, digging in with her sharp fingers. "Don't tell me you've forgotten."

'"Are you mad?" I said slowly. "You said yourself she never existed, or if she did she must have died a hundred years ago!"

'"Well, she's alive, and she's certainly not a wrinkled old crone, and she's upstairs at this very minute."

'"Listen," I told her, taking her by the shoulders, "I believe that there is a Mrs Clarke upstairs — Clarke is a common name, isn't it? — I'll even believe that she's a British spy. But surely . . ."

'"I know it's *the* Mrs Clarke because she spoke to me," Lucy interrupted. "She asked me for the parcel."

'At this I felt a *frisson* go up my spine, and it wasn't just the draughts in the chilly cloakroom. Eventually I managed to get a coherent story out of Lucy. At teatime she had been sent for by Mother to hand round the cakes and sandwiches, something that she quite often did. That was how she came to hear the stories about Russia and the Balkans. On her rounds afterwards she came up to Mrs Clarke, who at that moment was standing on her own looking out of the drawing-room window. Instead of helping herself to a cake, she drew Lucy close and said, in a low voice, *"I believe you have a parcel for me, haven't you?"*

'Lucy got such a fright that she nearly dropped the plate, and could only gawp. Then she saw Lady Tullich swimming over towards them, and Mrs Clarke had just time to whisper: "Get it ready for me in half an hour — I may need help in leaving the house unobserved," before she was enveloped in Lady T's great fur-clad bosom. Lu wriggled away, and a few minutes later she saw Mrs Clarke beckoning to her. It was getting dark by this time

33

and Morris had just come in to draw the curtains and light the lamps. Mrs Clarke leaned down and said: "You and your brother shouldn't have opened that box, you know. You have drawn much danger towards yourselves, and I must remove it immediately." Then she told Lucy to look out of the side window, but not to let herself be seen, and tell her if there was anything unusual in the street below.

'Lu slipped behind the curtain and peered down. The lamp opposite had been lit, and shed a dim, shuttered bluish light through the snow. And a few yards from that, looking up at our house, was the Captain. Of course, we didn't know him by that name then, it was what we were told later. But Lucy said it was the same sinister figure we had seen on that strange afternoon so many months ago, at the mouth of the close.

'At her description I felt a sudden lurch of fear. She asked me if I had noticed anything as I came in, but of course I had seen nothing.

'"Did you — get out the parcel?" I asked, trying to keep my voice steady. She nodded, and led the way into the schoolroom. On the table was the parcel, wrapped in anonymous brown paper.

'There were voices on the upstairs landing, my Mother's and another which was unfamiliar to me. And yet, I had the odd feeling that I had heard it somewhere before.

'It was a low, charming voice, unaccented, but with a faint foreign intonation I could not place. It was as if English was not the speaker's mother tongue, no matter how fluently she spoke it. She was saying something to Mother about not breaking up the party, and not to bother to see her out. "I must slip away quietly. Your charming children will see me out — I see them there below."

'Mother called to me, and I went to be introduced. I was instructed to help Mrs Clarke, for of course it was she, in every possible way — what about calling a cab? If it had not been for the Commissioner, she herself would have . . . (and, in the fuss of protestations and goodbyes, I had time to wonder whether Mrs

Clarke herself arranged the good Colonel's visit, for nothing short of a Red Cross Commissioner would normally have prevented Mother from seeing a guest of honour to the door). So Mother retired to the drawing-room, and I was able to get a good look at Mrs Clarke for the first time.

'Again I had the strange conviction that I knew her; that it wasn't by a long chalk the first time I had seen her. And then I realised. When I was very small I had an imaginary — companion. I called her Lalla. I pretended that she came and kissed me goodnight. She wasn't stern and distant like Mother, but absolutely gorgeous. She was very beautiful, with huge violet coloured eyes, and the most wonderful red-gold hair that coiled round and round her head up to a point on top. She was always dressed in floaty silks and chiffons, caught in at the breast with flowers — orchids and roses, some that I couldn't even name. And she smelt marvellous, like spring flowers. But it was that extraordinary hair that I remembered most. I'd only once seen anything like it — a little terra-cotta figurine in a museum. Much later I found that it came from the Minoan civilisation of Crete — thousands of years ago. Well, here, coming towards me — smiling at me on the landing — was Lalla. Mrs Clarke *was* Lalla.

'She wasn't wearing a floating dress, but was in the height of fashion, a dark red velvet suit with a long tunic over a narrow skirt to her ankles. A tall fur hat covered her hair. She carried a fur-trimmed coat, which she held out to me, and I helped her into it.

'"Thank you, Harry dear," she smiled at me. "And now — the parcel if you please!" So Lucy, all stares, handed it to her. She picked up from the hall chair an enormous muff, matching the hat, with long tails of fur hanging from it, and thrust the parcel inside. Then she whipped out her gloves, put them on and buttoned them briskly. "And now, dear children, the back entrance, if you please."

'We ushered her through the schoolroom. I raised the curtain and looked out into the snowy garden. Then, without thinking of coat or galoshes, I unbolted the window. Lucy handed me the

35

torch. "Keep guard!" I said to her. I ran down the iron steps and turned, shining my torch for her. She seemed to glide down behind me. Then she took my hand and we positively skimmed over the drying green and between the redcurrant bushes until we came to the gate in the back wall. Usually it was the devil to open, but that night the bolt just slid back as though it had been oiled. We came out into the little lane which leads to Brechin Gardens. As she bent to kiss me I smelt violets.

"'I will tell you again what I have already told your sister. You were very unwise to open the casket. Something evil has been drawn towards you by that act. However, now that I have it safe their interest may well be averted from you. Do you have any idea what the ..." she paused, then went on smoothly "... the *substance* is?" I shook my head, staring at her. I was so excited I could hardly take in what she was saying. Something about the war between the Forces of Light and the Forces of Darkness, that had gone on for thousands of years. Then she said that she was going to "hold us in the light" — an odd expression I thought, and that we were to pray for her that night as she was in danger and had to take the casket to a safe place. There was more — some reference to "The Knights", whoever *they* were. Then she put her hand on my head for a moment and I had the most extraordinary feeling, standing by the gate in that dark snowy garden — as though the sun had come from behind a cloud and was pouring down on top of me. It only lasted for a moment, but I felt calm and sort of glowing afterwards. I watched her turn and walk away from me through the snow.

'When I got back to the window Lucy was quite agitated. She had heard Father calling for me. Together we brushed the snow out of my hair and off my jacket, but of course my feet were sopping wet, and that was the first thing Father noticed when he came in. I said I had just stepped outside for a minute, but I got the usual lecture and was bundled straight off to have a mustard bath. Mouncie got ticked off too; although she was Lucy's governess she was supposed to keep an eye on us both, and that put *her* in a mood.

'So what with one thing and another, I didn't have a chance to tell Lucy what Mrs C had said, *or* look out for anybody who might be watching the house — or even pray for her as she'd asked me, until much later on when I was in bed. By that time, of course, I had the feeling that it must be too late, and I felt the most dreadful sense of guilt, like a stone weighing on my chest.

'The next morning we heard the news. It was a Saturday and too wet for us to be out, so we were quarrelling over a rather boring game of Halma. Mother came into the schoolroom and drew Mouncie over by the window where she spoke in a low voice. Mouncie gave a little shriek, and then glanced over at us. "How dreadful," she exclaimed. "An accident, I suppose?" We pricked up our ears at this. There was more whispering, and I heard the word "hospital".

'Then Mother left the room and Mouncie, who was still annoyed with me, told me sharply to let my sister alone. We knew where to get our information from, though. Lucy slipped down to the kitchen shortly afterwards, on the pretext of asking Morris to bring more coal for the fire. When she came back I could see from her expression that something momentous had happened, and when Mouncie was out of the room a few minutes later, she told me what she had learned from the maids.

'Mrs Clarke had been knocked down by a car on the approach to Waverley station the night before. It was thought that she had been hurrying to catch the night express to London. The car did not stop, but passers-by who saw the accident rushed to her help, an ambulance was called, and she was taken to the Royal Infirmary where she was gravely ill. Whether she still had the Casket or not we had no means of telling.

'I was devastated by the news — far more than Lucy, who I think was quite excited by all the commotion. How I blamed myself for not having thought of her, prayed for her earlier. I even eavesdropped on my parents. "She was carrying important documents," my father said. "I understand she was taking them

37

to London, to the Foreign Office. And these were stolen as she lay in the gutter." I wondered if he was talking about the box hidden in her muff. Rumours abounded — she was dying — she was much better — the accident had been engineered by German spies — and then at last we heard that she had been moved to Lady Tullich's house where she was convalescing. And then my Mother called to enquire after her, and apparently she asked especially that "dear Harry and Lucy" should pay her a visit.

'I walked on air for the rest of that week. Mouncie and Lucy kept teasing me that I had a crush on Mrs Clarke. I agonised over whether to take her flowers, at the last moment spending my meagre pocket money on a little bunch of snowdrops tied in ivy. Even now I remember how excited I was as we reached Lady Tullich's house. It was one of those big Edwardian edifices out at Colinton, quite new and rather grand in its large garden, with a splendid conservatory out at the back, and how convenient for school I thought.

'I could hardly speak as we were ushered into her room. Lady Tullich had given her a pretty little drawing-room on the first floor, with an adjoining bedroom reached through double doors. There was a fire burning, and she was lying on a chaise longue in front of it, propped up on a mass of silky cushions. Behind her, on a polished table, was a great bank of flowers — pots of rose azaleas, white hyacinths, narcissi, daffodils, iris, early hothouse tulips. I held out my pathetic little bunch of snowdrops with embarrassment, but she held them to her face and smiled her thanks as if they had been rare orchids. She was wearing a soft, pale-coloured blouse, I remember, with ruffles of lace round the wrists and at the neck. She wore no jewellery, apart from a narrow gold chain which had hanging from it a strangely shaped pendant — a sort of star. This she fingered from time to time. She was very pale, with a sort of translucent look, like moonstones. Her hair, which I saw now in all its glory for the first time, was a wonderful red-gold, just as I remembered it. A shaft of wintry sunshine, breaking through the window, touched it and made it burn.

'I don't remember how I choked down my tea, or what was said, but after a while Lady Tullich took Mother and Lucy off to her conservatory to cut some flowers, and I was left alone with her. But I do remember every word she said to me then, speaking faintly, for she was still weak, but with great urgency.

'"I am going away in a few days, Harry," she told me. "And I may never return, for the work I am doing is dangerous. It is a much older conflict than fighting Germans, a million ages have seen this war. And you — whether you like it or not — are involved in it now. You are very young, but for that reason I must trust you. Be on your guard at all times." Then she told me about the Captain, as she called him, and his ship, the *Nostradamus*, and how, for centuries now, he had been in pursuit of one thing, the mysterious substance in the box, which she told me was called the Martlet Casket. The birds engraved on it were not swallows, as I had thought, but martlets, heraldic birds like swifts without feet, which a magic significance.

'Then we heard Mother and Lady Tullich talking as they came up the stairs, and Lalla, as I now thought of her, reached out for my hand. Into it she put something small and hard, with a cold, metallic feel. Before I could look she had closed my fingers round it, and covered my hand with her own.

'"You must keep this always close to you, never let it be seen and never, never tell anyone about it. Think of it as a talisman, only to be used if you are in great danger." I felt a power like fire pass from her hands to mine. She spoke rapidly, in a low voice.

'"Even before I parted with you that night I knew that carrying what I did had brought great danger upon me. There was a motor waiting for me at the foot of the avenue, but I did not want to bring that danger upon others, so I hailed a passing cab and directed it to take me to Waverley Station. I had a reservation for the night sleeper to London. In the darkness of the cab I unlocked the box, using the secret catch. You may have realised that there is such a virtue in the metal and the magic design upon it that once inside the box nobody can manipulate the — let us call it the substance, it has another name, but it is better that you do not know it. With all the force of my will I sent that substance to the only safe place I knew of, to await recovery. Somehow, I sensed that I was being followed, so I left the cab in Princes Street and made my way to the station on foot, hoping to elude my pursuers; I have various little — strategems" (there she smiled faintly) "by which I can normally deceive the eye, but that night I was unsuccessful. Still, all they got was the empty casket."

'I wanted to ask her questions, but at that moment Lady Tullich, Mother and Lucy (who was looking cloudy and jealous) came into the room. Quickly, without looking at it, I transferred the object she had given to me into my trousers' pocket. There was a great deal of fuss about how I had tired dear Mrs Clarke out, and indeed she was looking very white and ill as she lay back on her cushions with her eyes closed. But she insisted on kissing me goodbye, and as I looked into her face, knowing I might never see her again, I had such a sense of loss, of desolation, that I felt a disgraceful sob come bursting up under my collar. Without speaking, I burst out of the room, ran down the stairs, out of the house, and down the drive. It was not until then, sniffling and choking in the shrubbery down by the gate, waiting for the wrath that I knew was coming, that I put my hand into my pocket for my handkerchief and drew out the object she had given me. It was a little key, silver by the look of it, curiously engraved. Somehow I knew what it was. It was the key to the Martlet Casket.'

In the silence that followed, Simon looked up.

'Well — go on.'

'There isn't any more. Nothing but blank pages.'

'Well, it makes a good story.' Simon stretched, catlike. 'I'd quite like to hear how it ends up. We obviously aren't going to get any more out of the old boy — why don't we take up his suggestion and phone Gran up? She might fill in the details.'

'You wouldn't say that if you knew Grandma,' Malcolm said gloomily. Nevertheless he brightened. 'Still, she's a good cook, unlike Ada. Wonder if she'd invite us to supper?'

Their grandmother sounded pleased to hear from them and an invitation to tea that afternoon was extended. As she had no car, they would have to make their own way to her, but it was a simple journey, and now that the snow had stopped, and the sun had come out, the two boys were eager to set off. Under Ada's disapproving gaze they gulped down their lunch of cold ham, pickled beetroot and potato salad; grabbed scarves and anoraks, and were out of the house within the hour. By unspoken mutual consent there was no further discussion of Uncle Henry's strange story.

CHAPTER FIVE

It wasn't until Malcolm and Simon were settled on the top of a number 23 bus, hurtling down the Canonmills, that the subject was raised again.

'Did Aunty Cath ever mention anything about all this?'

Malcolm knew what 'all this' meant. He looked uncomfortable.

'Ma always treats Uncle H as a bit of a joke, to be honest. When Daddy was alive we used to have him to stay occasionally, and we'd always look him up when we came to Edinburgh. But recently, since we moved down to London and Ma got that job . . . well, we just haven't seen much of him for a year or so. In fact, if that skiing holiday of yours hadn't fallen through at the last moment when your parents were just about to leave for Kenya, and Ma had to be rushed into hospital for appendicitis — well, this is the last place either family would think of sending us.'

'As a matter of fact, I'm quite enjoying it.' Simon remarked. 'He's not a bad old stick, and he lets us do pretty much as we like. I think the general idea in our family is that he's harmlessly cuckoo. What's Gran like, by the way? Laurie called on her a couple of times and quite liked her.' Laurie was Simon's eldest brother who had just finished at Edinburgh University. There was another brother and sister, both in their late teens. They were all very brainy — in fact, Malcolm, who had only met them once, at his father's funeral, found them all quite intimidating.

'Oh, she's OK — a bit bossy. You've met her before though.'

'Not since I was a kid. I remember she came to stay with us

once, when we were in Paris. I didn't see much of her. And, of course, she came with Uncle H. to the airport when I arrived, but she didn't stay very long.'

'Well, you can judge for yourself in a minute. Here's our stop.'

Their grandmother lived in Goldenacre, on the other side of the city, in a terrace of neat Victorian houses. Each one had a square front garden, with a straight, stone-flagged path leading to the front door. As they opened the gate, Simon enquired:

'She and Uncle Henry have quarrelled, haven't they? She was awfully stiff with him that day I arrived — and he kept hrrmphing and ignoring her. What's it all about, do you know?'

But before Malcolm could reply, their grandmother, who had obviously been watching for their arrival, had opened the front door.

'I just spoke to your mother, Malcolm,' were her first words. 'She's making a very good recovery; the hospital are going to let her go home at the end of the week, and she's going to stay with Mrs Carr for a few days. They offered to have you too, but I said you were doing just fine where you were.'

Malcolm was relieved to hear this; although he missed his mother the idea of staying in the Carrs' house, which was a tiny Regency villa in Twickenham, filled with precious furniture and antique carpets, made him shudder. He plied his grandmother with further questions as they were ushered into her cosy sitting-room. Tea was spread out on a low table by the fire; hot scones, homemade cherry jam, a chocolate cake that looked as if it came out of a magazine advertisement, and a great pile of buttered toast. When they had finished, their grandmother settled back in her armchair with her knitting, while her old terrior, Joss, lay down on her feet. She was a small, neatly dressed woman, with sandy-grey hair carefully waved. Her eyes, behind her glasses, were sharp. She studied Simon.

'You're a lot like your mother,' she said at last. 'That brother of yours favours your father. A clever lad, though. He gets it from his grandfather. You never met him, either of you, but my dear husband was a brilliant man. Brilliant.' She sighed, clicked her needles. Simon seized his opportunity.

'I thought Uncle Henry was supposed to have been quite brilliant, too, in his own way. Didn't he have a first class honours degree in chemistry or something?'

'Oh, *Henry*,' Mrs Frazer said in a dismissive tone. 'Henry was just a flash in the pan. It's lucky he got left all that money from his godfather. He could never stick at anything. And when Mother died and he inherited that gloomy house — well, he just shut himself up there with those silly experiments of his . . .'

'Didn't he build a laboratory in the back garden that got burned down in a mysterious fire about six years ago?'

'There was nothing mysterious about that fire, I can tell you. He used to have an old oil stove in there in the winter, and a stray cat got in when he had left the door open one day, knocked it over, and up the whole ramshackle thing went. Lucky he wasn't in there at the time.'

'Do you know what his experiments were about, Gran?' Simon pursued. 'Could they have been something to do with recreating a strange substance, a substance that could change its shape and travel through solid objects, but looked like a little blob of beaten egg-white . . .?'

His grandmother put down her knitting. She looked cross.

'Don't tell me he's been filling your heads with all that claptrap!' she exclaimed sharply. 'Fairy story nonsense! He ought to know better at his age.'

'We thought you might be able to give us your side of the story, Gran,' Malcolm said. His grandmother straightened her back, looked around her neat, cheerful room, as though to draw confidence from it, and picked up her needles again. A fat, striped footstool of a cat, called Peter, attempted to jump onto her lap. She brushed him to the floor.

'There's a place for cats,' she told him, 'but not on a knitting lap, as you well know.'

Peter gave her a look which boded no good, and leapt on the

back of the sofa, where he listened with interest, and apparent understanding, to the discussion.

'You'd better tell me exactly what your Great-Uncle Henry has told you. Then I'll let you know if there's any truth in it.'

So the boys related the entire story, up to the finding of the key, exactly as they had heard it. When they had finished, Mrs Frazer sighed again. She was a long time in speaking, when she did so it was with reluctance.

'As you know, your mothers, Cathy and Liz, are my only children. Neither of them were — what you might call imaginative when they were young. They were clever girls, especially Liz. She took after your grandfather, and — like him — wanted to be a doctor. She got a good degree too, could have had a career if she hadn't married your father. And your mother, Malcolm, with her gift for maths — look how well she's doing with that computer company she works for now. Anyway, even when they were babies they never cared much for fairy stories, magic, that kind of thing. When they were about your age, maybe a little younger, your Uncle Henry made the mistake of telling that tarradiddle about Mrs Clarke and the Martlet Casket. It wouldn't have been so bad if he'd pretended it was a fantasy, but they said he tried to convince them it was true. Well, Cathy got a fit of the giggles, and Liz just thought he was clean gyte — mad, as we say.

'So, when they came to me with the tale, I had to have my version of events quite pat. That Henry had always been highly strung, that he had had a nervous breakdown as a young man (that part was quite true) that they had to be kind and tolerant because, well, because he was — *not really all there*.' This last bit was said in a whisper very unlike Mrs Frazer's usual sharp tones.

'You mean,' Malcolm burst out, 'that you told our mothers he had imagined it all, except, perhaps, Mrs Clarke, and that all the stuff about the box was nonsense. You made out that he was telling a load of lies — and was mad into the bargain! You lied to them!'

He was red in the face, and his voice had risen almost to a shout.

He was so agitated that he had quite forgotten the precept that one should never be rude to one's elders, and Simon thought that his grandmother was going to be very angry. Surprisingly, she took the outburst meekly enough, telling him quietly to sit down again.

'You're angry with me, I know, and maybe you've a right to be. But I still think it was *something that had to be done at the time*. I was going to tell you the same story, but somehow I felt that I wanted to tell the truth after all this time. Not that I'm too sure of the truth any more.'

Malcolm muttered something under his breath and Simon, surprisingly, turned on him. 'Don't be so childish, Malc.' It was the first time he had used the diminutive. 'Did you think that grown-ups never tell lies?'

Their grandmother rose and went to draw the curtains against the sad end of the day. It was not snowing, but the sky was a dark, lowering grey. The lamps were already lit.

'Of course,' she said, slowly, 'I never trusted that Mrs Clarke. Not after the first meeting anyway. Yes, Malcolm, she did exist. And we did have that strange adventure in the Old Town that afternoon before Christmas. Lord knows I've tried, but I've never been able to find a logical explanation for it. And I do remember playing around with that odd gauzy stuff in the carved box — but how much of that was real and how much a childhood fantasy I just cannot tell.'

'Is that why you and Uncle Henry aren't on speaking terms? Because you made him out to be a loony?'

'I didn't exactly say he was a loony, Simon. But yes, it has caused a rift between us. And I have had to stand by and watch him wasting his life. I blame it all on that woman. She cast a sort of spell over him. He was never the same after he met her.'

'Why don't you come over and visit him?' Malcolm suggested. He seemed to have recovered his good humour. 'It might be easier while we're there.'

'You could tell him you're sorry,' Simon put in.

'I might. It wouldn't be easy though. Still, I suppose I owe it to

46

him. I'll ring him tomorrow. Poor old Henry. And now you ought to be going, or he'll start worrying on about you. If you bring me your coats, I'll warm them in front of the fire.'

When this had been done, she saw them to the front door.

'You know, once I thought I saw Mrs Clarke again. It was in the spring of 1944, just before the end of the last war. We were living in Morningside then, and your mothers must have been about ten and twelve years old. In fact it was shortly after there had been all that nonsense about Henry's story. The girls had just started music lessons and I was looking down the road for them from an upstairs window. It was five o'clock — they were a bit late and I was beginning to worry. And then, out of the corner of my eye, I saw, or rather, sensed, someone come up the path to the front door. I looked down, and for an instant I saw her, before she passed under the porch. I hurried down to the front door — there was no one there, so I ran down the path and opened the gate. There was nobody in the road either. It was still evening; I remember the yellow crocuses were out. And then Cathy and Liz came round the corner, dragging their music cases and giggling. When they reached me, Liz said, "What's the matter, mum, you look as though you'd seen a ghost!" I almost told them that I had — but I thought better of it and gave them a ticking off for not being home on time. But I couldn't forget it. I knew it was her. She looked exactly the same — red velvet suit and all. I wondered why she'd come, and if she'd ever come back, but she never did. I never mentioned it to your uncle, we weren't on very good terms by then.'

Their grandmother gave a little shiver and pulled her cardigan closer.

'Ff, it's cold in this hall. Now hurry home, both of you, and I promise I'll ring in the morning. You know where to get the bus, don't you?'

They assured her that they did.

'Don't tell your parents what I've told you. They'll think I'm mad too. Best to put it all out of your minds. Anyway, it couldn't have been Mrs Clarke that I saw. We heard months later that she had been killed in a train accident, somewhere abroad I think it was. I remember Mother being very upset.'

She watched them out of the garden gate; then the square of light from her front door was cut off. It was misty-dark. Frost made halos round the lamps. The boys stepped out briskly over thin, crunching snow.

'Cross over here.'

They glanced behind them as they crossed. A shadow took form on the pavement opposite — a tall shape, hatted, long-coated, leaning a little in the lamplight.

They turned back, running.

There was nothing. An angle of wall, a cotoneaster bush, a pointed reflection from the lamp-post.

Imagination?

CHAPTER SIX

When they arrived back they were met at the front door by Ada. She told them, in a voice which implied they were responsible, that their great-uncle was not feeling well and had retired to bed. She also informed them that young Bina Henderson from next door had been round again, and had asked them over tomorrow. They could phone her if they liked.

'I'll ring her now,' said Malcolm.

When he returned from the telephone, Simon was curled up in an armchair in the study with his nose in a book.

'We're to go round for lunch and watch the Scotland-Ireland international on their television in the afternoon.'

'Great,' said Simon unenthusiastically. He did not care very much for rugby football. 'You know, we never got round to asking Gran whether Uncle H had told her about the key — or even if they heard again from the mysterious Mrs Clarke.'

'Well, she did say that they had heard about Mrs Clark being killed in a train crash some months afterwords, so it looks as if that was the end of the matter — except for the odd little ghost story about her appearing at the door one Spring evening. Very unlike Grandma, that, she's normally so down-to-earth and sensible. Of course if anything else did happen when they were children it's possible she may not have known about it — she obviously didn't care too much for Mrs C — particularly after Uncle developed such a crush on her.'

'Yes — that's why it's so strange that Mrs C should have appeared to Gran and not him that day; assuming that it's true, of course,' Simon added hastily.

'Let's ask Uncle Henry some more questions tomorrow, if he's better. Ada said he had a feverish cold and she was going to call the doctor, but she does fuss over him.'

'I wish there was a TV set here,' Simon sighed. 'It's not as though he can't afford one.'

'He thinks it rots the brain — and for heaven's sake don't bring the matter up in front of him, or we'll be in for another of those long reminiscences about what they did for entertainment when he was a child. Anyway, we can pop over to the Hendersons and watch theirs if there's anything good on.'

'Ah yes, the Hendersons. This Bina seems to be quite keen on you. What's she like? Pretty?' Simon peered at his cousin over his glasses in the manner of a well-known television commentator. Malcolm reddened slightly.

'I've told you before — I hardly know her. When I got here, before you arrived, her family asked me over, I expect they thought I was bored here on my own. She's OK for a girl. Clever, but a good sense of humour. I suppose she's quite pretty — I never really thought about it. She's rather bossy — that I can tell you.'

And with that brief description, Simon had to be content. He had learned by now that Malcolm could be very stubborn.

After they had finished supper they played Scrabble for an hour or so in front of the study fire, and were just about to go to bed yawning, when they were both jerked awake by a sharp clanging noise. As they looked at each other it sounded again. It echoed through the house, dying away into nothing.

Ada, white as her apron, burst into the room.

'Who rang that bell? Which of you boys is it that's daured tae play games wi' a bell that hasnae rung in thirty years?'

They ran into the hall, into the back passage inside the kitchen door. A row of bells hung above their heads. One still danced like a mad puppet.

'If either of you two . . .'

'But, Ada! The wires — look, they're rusted away!'

Ada moaned. 'Guid sakes!'

Even as she spoke, the bell began to swing again, tattering silence with tinny clangour — the infection spread down the line until all seven bells jinked, twirled, jangled together in an infernal fandango. Mesmerised, they stared — and leapt as they heard a noise behind them. It was Uncle Henry, wrapped in a capacious woollen dressing-gown, an eiderdown around his shoulders.

'Boys, Ada, what on earth is going on?'

'Mr Gilchrist, sir, I'm no' answering *that*!'

'I'll go,' volunteered Malcolm.

'I'll come with you.' Simon was not to be outdone.

They threw open the front door.

There was nobody in the dark roadway, up or down.

Ada was whimpering. She threw her apron over her head.

'All right, Ada, all right,' Mr Gilchrist told her. He cleared his throat. 'It was obviously something in the atmosphere — frost in the air. Be a good woman and make me a cup of tea. I've got a bad enough chill as it is, without traipsing around in a cold hall in my dressing-gown. I'm going back to my bed.'

Ada moved in a trance back to her kitchen. The boys remained for a few minutes, staring at the bells. Dead still they hung now, as though never a clapper had tolled since the electric circuit had been put in, more than a generation ago. Not an echo hung in the air.

They went back to the study, and sat down again in front of the fire.

'Of course, there's some perfectly logical explanation for it.' Simon rubbed the bridge of his nose. He had taken off his glasses and looked oddly vulnerable without them. 'It probably *is* something in the atmospheric conditions — like those electric burglar alarms that go off for no reason.'

'There's something I haven't told you,' Malcolm said. He sounded unusually serious. 'I didn't think you'd believe me, but

51

now . . . well, I suppose I'll have to trust you. You remember when I went up to our bedroom to get my jersey about half an hour ago; well, when I reached the half-landing window something made me stop and look out. I don't know why. The curtains weren't drawn and the light wasn't on at the top part of the stairs. I could see right across the road because the moon was so bright. And I saw — *him*!'

'That was just your imagination. Remember how we both thought we saw something outside Gran's house, but it was only a shadow? Anyway, why didn't you come and get me to have a look?'

'Because I knew exactly what you would say — that it was just a trick of the moonlight.' Malcolm got to his feet. 'I knew you wouldn't believe me. But I'll tell you one thing for sure — that bell ringing tonight was not due to some change in the atmosphere.'

'Well — if it was the Captain ringing then why wasn't he on the doorstep waiting to be let in?' Simon laughed, although for some reason he didn't find this particularly funny.

Malcolm shuddered. 'I'm jolly glad he wasn't,' he said. 'I'm going to bed. Coming?'

Simon wanted to finish the chapter he had been reading earlier and said he would follow in ten minutes. Yes, he would remember to switch off the fire. A few minutes later he heard the door to their bedroom close. It was very quiet in the room, Ada must have gone to bed as there was no sound from the kitchen. A clock ticked. Somehow, Simon found it hard to concentrate, but he managed to plough through two pages without really taking in the sense of the words. He put the book down, switched off the fire and the light. Malcolm had left the upper landing light on, but the hall and first flight of stairs were in semi-darkness. When he reached the landing, something impelled him to look out. Nothing.

Then something, some slight movement below, made him look directly down. What he saw so terrified him that he thought for a moment he was going to faint. Immediately below him, and looking directly up at the window, was a face. He only saw it for a fraction of a second, then it seemed to dissolve into shadows, but he could never forget it.

It was a very pale face; not white but an unhealthy greyish colour. He could see the features quite clearly, except for the eyes which were shaded under the brim of a dark hat. The cheeks were flabby, the mouth small, with a distinctly unpleasant expression.

Simon's first instinct was to duck back. When he looked again he saw nothing. As swiftly as he could, he ran up the rest of the stairs and burst into the bedroom he shared with his cousin. Malcolm's reading lamp was on. He was propped up on one elbow.

'What on earth's up — you look awful!'

Simon sat down on his own bed. 'I've just seen the Captain.' His voice, in spite of his efforts to control it, was shaking. 'He was standing by the front door, looking up at the half-landing window. Then he just — disappeared.'

Malcolm brought him a glass of water, which he drank gratefully.

'Of course, it could have been a burglar, in which case I seem to have scared him off. I hope all the doors and windows downstairs are locked.' Simon was beginning to recover his poise.

'No,' Malcolm said decisively. 'It was the Captain all right. I saw him too, remember. He's after something, but I wish I knew what it was. And I don't think he can get inside this house — otherwise he'd have done it before. Something in this house is protecting us, and I'm pretty sure that whatever it is is what he wants, or is linked to it in some way. The puzzle is — what is it?'

They both thought for a minute. Then Simon jumped up, his face tense with excitement.

'I've got it — I know what it is! It's the key — the key to the Martlet Casket or whatever it's called. The one Uncle Henry was given when he was a boy!'

'But we don't even know if he's still got it.'

'Of course he has — don't forget that his beloved Mrs Clarke told him to guard it with his life, and that it would *save him from danger if necessary*. I'll bet you anything you like that it's in that desk in his bedroom — the one that used to belong to Great-grandma Gilchrist.'

'Well, we can't get it now,' Malcolm said sensibly. 'We'd better get some sleep and have it out with him in the morning.'

'I can't possibly sleep,' Simon said, 'knowing that he's out there in the garden.' He got into bed, however, and pulled the eiderdown up under his chin. To his surprise, he found himself yawning. Malcolm was very stolid and reassuring.

'Did you ever mention any of this to what's her name — Bina?' he asked sleepily.

'Yes, as a matter of fact I did. She laughed, but she asked me a lot of questions. I think she was interested really, but didn't want to show it.'

'Perhaps we should tell her what happened today,' Simon yawned. He was almost asleep.

'I don't see why not. As long as she doesn't make a joke of it. Uncle's got a soft spot for her, so she might be able to get him to tell us where he put the key. Anyway, we'll sound her out tomorrow. 'Night.'

''Night.'

Malcolm lay awake for a while, turning things over in his mind. When he did sleep it was to dream that he was in a large room, heavily panelled in a dark, shiny wood, with heavy cherry-red velvet curtains, a thick carpet with an oriental pattern, and a large marble fireplace in which a fire burned cheerfully. He was sitting on an overstuffed Victorian sofa and facing him, on a low, quilt-backed chair, was a woman he knew beyond doubt was Mrs Clarke. She was leaning forward and talking to him earnestly, but he could not make out a word she was saying. At last, in apparent exasperation, she took hold of his shoulders and shook him, but as she did so he woke up to find Simon, fully dressed, pulling back his bedclothes and telling him to hurry up, or he would be late for breakfast.

CHAPTER SEVEN

After breakfast Ada insisted on calling the doctor, who pronounced that Uncle Henry had a bad cold which was turning to bronchitis. He prescribed antibiotics and a stay in bed, in the warm. True to her word, their grandmother rang up, and although she could not speak to her brother, it was arranged, with the boys as intermediaries, that she should call that evening.

It was a fine morning; the sun was shining on yesterday's thin snow, which had not yet melted. Malcolm put his head round his uncle's bedroom door to find out if he wanted anything. It was a large room, the double windows looking out over the front garden. Uncle Henry lay, propped up on pillows, in a big double bed with brass knobs. There was a stuffy smell of Friar's Balsam and cough linctus.

'We're sorry you're ill, Uncle.'

Uncle Henry wheezed.

'Just a bit tight in the chest. It'll pass, it'll pass.'

Simon joined them, wandering over to the window. He ran his hand over the desk as he passed.

'We read that story you gave us, sir. It was extremely interesting. In fact, we checked it out with Grandma and she told us it was all true.'

(This was a slight exaggeration, but one that Simon felt was justified.)

Uncle Henry raised himself higher on his pillows. His face was red.

'Now, listen here young fellow. You had absolutely no right to go discussing things with . . .'

'We also think we saw the Captain yesterday,' Simon interrupted him.

His uncle sat bolt upright, as if galvanised.

'What — what — *where?*' he spluttered.

'Once outside Grannie's house, as we were leaving. And we both saw him last night, watching this house.'

'We think he's after something. Something that you have. In fact we think he could be after the key to the Martlet Casket. Have you still got it?'

'Got it? Of course I've got it. It's locked in my desk, there.'

The two boys exchanged glances.

'Can we see it?' Simon asked.

'Presently. Not just now.'

'Did you ever see her again — Mrs Clarke, I mean?' Simon wanted confirmation.

Their uncle shook his head.

'Six months later we heard that she'd been killed in a train crash. Somewhere in the Balkans. I never believed that report.'

'But Uncle, if she's still alive she must be a very old lady by now. Over a hundred years old.'

Uncle Henry regarded Simon with dislike.

'She is ageless,' he said with dignity. 'In a sense she is immortal.'

The doorbell, unmistakably electric this time, sounded below.

'I can't imagine who that is. I don't feel up to visitors just now.'

But there was no time to answer, for Ada's voice was heard as she opened the door, then, flying footsteps up the stairs. There was a knock, and a tall slim girl of about thirteen entered, bearing a bunch of daffodils and narcissi.

'Bina!' the old man exclaimed, sounding pleased.

'Mother sent you these.' She came towards him, laid the flowers down on the bedside table. 'She's very sorry to hear you're not well — we all are — and if there's any messages I'm to do them. Hullo, Malcolm! And I suppose this is Simon.'

She was not pretty, but her smile, gay and compassionate, lit up her rather long, pale face. She was obviously on good terms with Uncle Henry.

'I'm taking these boys out of your road this afternoon, Mr Gilchrist,' she said in a brisk voice. 'They can have lunch with us and then watch that boring rugby match on television. I loathe rugby myself, but I've plenty I can be going on with. In fact, they can come over now if they like.'

'That's very good of you and your mother, my dear. I am rather tired at the moment. I think I'll just have a little sleep. Go on, boys. You can come up and see me again at teatime. I might have something to show you then, but I want to think about it first.'

Uncle Henry closed his eyes, suddenly looking very old. The boys followed Bina Henderson out of the room. There was no more to be said just now.

***

The living-room of the house next door was bright and modern. After a good lunch (quite a contrast, as Simon disloyally remarked, to Ada's cooking) Bina's parents left them alone. They were going to visit friends and would not be back until five. Bina's elder sister was out shopping, so they had the house to themselves. The boys watched the match, and Bina sat at a table, tacking up a dress she had just cut out. She dropped her reel of cotton.

'Pick that up, there's a dear,' she ordered Malcolm, who obeyed instantly. 'He's my obedient slave, you know,' she told Simon.

'You might as well turn that thing off, since you're neither of you watching it,' she added sharply. 'You've been mooning about like a couple of idiots all day — what on earth is the matter? You'd better tell me.'

Malcolm needed very little prompting. When he had finished, Bina nicked off her thread with sharp teeth.

'So that's the whole story, is it? Un-believable!'

'It may seem unbelievable to you, but I can assure you we saw him.'

'There's no need to be so pompous, Malcolm. I'm not saying I don't believe you, but you must admit that it's a little hard to take. It's better than the library book I'm reading, all about the ghosties and ghoulies of old Edinburgh. Well, we'll have to keep a sharp lookout for him from now on. Tell me again what he looks like.'

Half an hour later, Bina looked at her watch with a little cry.

'Goodness, I must get to the supermarket before it shuts. I've some messages to do for Ma, and she'll murder me if she gets back and finds them not done. You two can come with me and carry my basket.'

They fetched their coats and in a few minutes were running down the avenue, muffled against the cold. The rain had cleared and the light was fading, leaving a dirty yellow rim on the edge of the sky behind high-rise flats and tall chimneys.

They crossed the road and entered the supermarket. Bina, Simon noticed, wasted no time shelf-gazing. She consulted the list in her hand, and went from shelf to shelf, selecting and dropping tins and packages into the wire basket which Malcolm held for her. They waited at the check-out and transferred the goods to a large straw bag. Out into the raw air, Bina handed over a last tin with the words 'Catch, slave!'

Malcolm staggered under the weight. 'We aren't your slaves,' he puffed. 'Give us a hand, Si.'

'Out of the goodness of my heart,' Simon concurred, 'but not because I am or ever will be a slave of yours, Bina Henderson.'

'Robina, *if* you please!'

They crossed over the road. It was almost dark. Street lights came on, sulphurous, yellow.

'You may be clever,' Bina remarked, 'but you have no eyes in your heads.' She handed out toffee.

'Meaning?'

'Someone in the supermarket. Watching — always in the next aisle. Hiding behind the soap powders.'

'Oh? Let's have a description.'

'The flick of a broad-brimmed hat. One eye in a pale face.'

'You're amazing. A pity you spoiled it with the bit about the soap powders.'

'I thought that was a nice touch. Don't you believe me?'

She looked from one to the other and burst out laughing, staggering so that she had to hold on to a lamp-post.

'You'll cry wolf once too often, Bina,' Malcolm said.

Carrying the bag between them, the boys led the way up the avenue. The dim orange light left pools of shadow across the road. Uphill, about fifty yards ahead, someone was crossing over to the far side. A tall figure, hatted, in a long dark coat. An oncoming car with headlights dipped hid him. When it had passed there was nobody.

They stopped, thrilled and yet uneasy.

'There are lots of gates he might have gone into . . .'

They raced uphill as best they could. Where the figure had been was a house in darkness. No proof either way. At the door of number twelve they parted, waiting to see Bina enter number thirteen. Ada was waiting.

'Your Grannie's here,' she announced. 'She's just arrived. I put her in the study. I don't know if Mr Gilchrist's well enough . . .'

'Of course he is, Ada!' said Malcolm. 'Go and tell — no, wait, we'll see her first.'

They hurried into the study, where Mrs Frazer and her dog, Joss, were sitting, very nervous, a basket full of fruit and a sponge cake at her side.

'Has the doctor been?' she asked, after preliminary greetings.

They assured her that all that was necessary was being done, and that their uncle was not dangerously ill.

She twisted her hands together. 'I doubt if he will see me, after all,' she murmured.

'He will. He's been longing to see you for ages, I'm positive,' Malcolm reassured her. 'Anyway, we told him you were coming, when you phoned this morning.'

Simon sat on the edge of her armchair. 'Gran,' he said. 'We've

59

seen the Captain. Last night, just after we'd left you, and later, watching this house. And we thought we saw him tonight, in the avenue.'

Their grandmother shook her head. 'He'd have no reason to come to *my* house. How did he look?'

Simon smiled. 'A shadow of his former self.'

She did not laugh.

'Gran,' Malcolm said, 'will you tell Uncle Henry what you told us yesterday — about seeing Mrs Clarke again?'

'I don't know, Malcolm; it would probably just upset him. I'll see how it goes.'

They had to be content with that for Ada came in and announced that Mrs Frazer could go up and see her brother now. She went slowly upstairs, leaving Joss with the boys.

The telephone rang. It was Bina. They told her that their grandmother was there, and of the conversation they had just had.

'I won't come over — I don't care for dogs. Listen, what I want to know is — have you seen this mysterious key of your uncle's yet?'

'No, we asked him this morning, and he said he might show it to us later. He's really not very well.'

'I've been thinking,' Bina said slowly. 'Time. That might be the answer, you know. She might have hidden the substance — that night she was trying to escape from them — by sealing it in some sort of time switch mechanism which will only release it when a certain set of circumstances are right. You know, I wonder if she hadn't intended it to be released in 1944 — that time your Grannie saw her — only the circumstances weren't right for some reason or other. Perhaps she found that your uncle was a failure and your Gran had put it all out of her mind — no that's not quite right. There's some other factor missing. Anyway, think about it. I'll see you tomorrow. Bye.' She rang off.

They weighed up her words, but could add nothing further.

'I think she's definitely got something there,' Simon mused. 'In that case, those circumstances must be present *now*; otherwise

60

why should the Captain reappear? And why only him? We've not seen a whisper of Mrs Clarke — not even a strand of red-gold hair!'

'Perhaps we have to call her — with the key, maybe?'

Joss barked as he heard their grandmother's voice. She looked much happier when she came into the room.

'I've told your uncle everything. It's a great weight off my chest. He's agreed to let bygones be bygones. Mind you, he was angry with me, but that's only natural. It's a great relief to have told him.' She fastened the lead to the dog's collar. 'Come, Joss.'

At the front door, she turned, made as if to speak, and then thought better of it. She drew on her gloves.

'If that Captain is back, my advice to you is on no account to follow him. Keep well out of his way and don't meddle with what you don't understand. And for God's sake — and your mothers' — don't set out on some silly quest like your uncle. You don't want to end up like him.'

She kissed them. 'Come and see me again soon. And if that woman, Mrs Clarke, turns up, see he doesn't run off with her to fairyland.'

CHAPTER EIGHT

There was no repetition of their sinister visitor that evening, but Ada told them severely that their uncle was not to be disturbed, as he was running a temperature and had been tired out by his sister's visit.

The next day, however, his illness seemed to take a turn for the better. He put away his Friar's Balsam inhaler and allowed the boys to come to his room after tea, where he sat, propped up on pillows, in an ancient, frogged Chinese silk dressing-jacket.

Spread upon a clean handkerchief on the eiderdown was the key. A curious, stumpy key, the pattern of the lock unusual, the handle a circled cross. It was brightly polished, and chased with a delicate pattern which had been worn faint with the years.

Simon examined it closely. 'Did you ever use it?'

'I had no lock to use it *in*, had I?' Uncle Henry rejoined testily. 'Besides, Mrs Clarke told me to keep it safe and only use it in case of great danger.'

'But how did you know when you'd be in great danger?' asked Malcolm. 'I mean, if you were out somewhere and suddenly got attacked or beaten up or something — well, it wouldn't be much use if the key were locked up here at home in your desk.'

'Originally, I wore it round my neck on a ribbon, under my vest, you know. But it made me itch, brought me out in a sort of rash.'

'Radioactive?'

'No, no! Though I must admit that, years later, I did test it with a Geiger counter. Absolutely negative reaction. It was probably just an allergy; I've always had very sensitive skin.' He coughed, reached for a glass of water on his bedside table. Simon turned the key over in his hands. It felt cold — rather more than normally so, perhaps?

'Did Mrs Clarke actually tell you it was the key to the Martlet Casket? You'd have thought she would have hung on to it until she got it back — the casket, I mean.'

'I don't think the key is crucial to the casket in that sense, though it may have been once. Look how easily I opened it by pressing the secret catch,' their uncle said. 'Anyway, it may well have been destroyed by now, remember that it was only of use to protect the substance. Once the Captain discovered that the box was empty — and it can't have taken him long to find out, even without the key — he probably got rid of it. Especially as he knew how important it was to Mrs Clarke and her people. They needed it in order to re-seal the substance inside it.'

'Yes, that's another thing we meant to ask you,' Simon said. 'Who are these mysterious people that Mrs Clarke talked about — the Knights that you mentioned? Did you ever find out?'

'And who was the Captain, really? You said he had a ship, the Nostra-something. Was he in the Navy?'

'He was — well, for want of a better word I suppose one could call him a pirate, although that always sounds rather jolly and he was anything but that. He was engaged in all sorts of nefarious activities, I did some research on him, later. Traced him through the ship. It was called the Nostradamus. Built in Holland around 1670, and captured in some fight — we were at war with the Dutch, on and off, for years at that time. Somehow or other, it ended up in Leith, in the middle of the eighteenth century, owned and commanded by a Captain Venner. I don't know how he got hold of it — it must have been a bit of a wreck by then. Anway, the authorities seemed to have turned a blind eye to him — they knew what he was up to — gun-running, smuggling, the slave trade and worse. He must have had friends in high places, or greased a few palms. Anyway, he came and went quite openly — had a big house in Leith, near the docks.'

'And he was — *the* Captain? You're sure of it?'

'Quite certain. Eventually his luck ran out, or someone turned on him. Anyway, in 1798 or so he was hauled up in front of the magistrates on a charge of murder and abduction. Some old man who kept what we call nowadays a junk shop. His body was found floating in the harbour, and someone left an anonymous message that a search should be made of the good Captain's house. Yes, yes, I know what you're thinking. It all fits in quite neatly, doesn't it?'

'Was he hanged?'

'I was coming to that. Well, they searched the Captain's house, and found the old man's hat, and a silver ring that belonged to him. However, there wasn't any motive that could be turned up. A contemporary pamphlet hinted that it was political — the French Revolution had erupted and there was a lot of unrest about. It's quite possible that the judge, or the jury, come to that, had been bribed. Anyway, the long and the short of it is that he got off. And he just disappeared — his ship too. Nobody ever saw hide nor hair of him again. But in my researches I came across a contemporary print, supposed to represent him as he stood at the dock. The moment I saw that I recognised him.'

'Have you got it now?' Simon asked excitedly.

'No, unfortunately; it was in a book that I lent to a friend of mine. When I asked for it back he searched the place thoroughly but found it had vanished. It wasn't a very good picture — a rather clumsy engraving, mainly showing the court in session. But you could see enough of him to know who it was.' Uncle Henry shuddered.

'And Mrs Clarke? And the Knights? Who were they?'

'I don't know — I can't think straight just now.' Uncle Henry clutched his head. 'This room is so stuffy, and I've got a dreadful headache. Leave me alone for a while and I'll talk to you again later. You might get Ada to make a hot lemon and honey drink if she has the time, and open that window a crack before you go.'

'Can we take the key with us?'

'Oh take it, take it, but for heaven's sake be careful with it. There's a little bag — yes, that's right, in the top drawer of the desk. Put the key in that, and you, Malcolm, hang it round your neck by that cord. Now be off with you.' He snuggled back into the bed, closing his eyes as the boys went quietly out.

They decided to call on Bina, but her elder sister, who answered the door, told them that she'd been taken by her parents on a trip to see her grannie who lived at Berwick. They left a message for her to ring them when she got back, but did not feel too hopeful that she would get it.

After lunch they decided to go to the cinema, and for nearly three hours completely forgot about sinister captains and mysterious boxes in the thrill of extra-terrestrial adventures. The lamps were lit as they walked back up the avenue in the twilight, but it was empty apart from two elderly women gossiping at a gate and an old man walking a dog. As they passed number thirteen, Bina's pretty, pink-haired sister came out giggling, clinging to her boyfriend's arm. She nodded curtly at them and was about to get into his car when she turned and called after them:

'I gave Bina your message — think she's round at your place now. She only went about three minutes ago.'

The car door slammed and they rushed up the path. Bina was just leaving — she had brought some fruit for their uncle. The boys hustled her into the living-room and reported their conversation with Uncle Henry. They showed her the key.

'It's quite pretty,' she said, examining it. She held it at arm's length in front of her. 'I wish that the beautiful red-haired Mrs Clarke would appear and — and . . .' she giggled. 'Nothing seems to have happened; you'll probably find that it's the key to the drinks cupboard or something! Anyway, I must go. Tell you what, why don't we do some researches of our own tomorrow. We could explore the Old Town — maybe go to the library and see if we could find that old print you were talking about — or visit the

65

Museum. I'll call for you just after lunch, I'm busy in the morning. See you!'

They knocked on Uncle Henry's door before supper, but he said that he was not feeling too good and would talk to them in the morning. However, from the glimpse they had of him, sitting up in bed with his silk dressing-jacket on, a large book propped on his lap, and what looked like the remains of a fairly substantial meal on the table at his side, he did not strike them as being very ill. And, in fact, at about nine o'clock, Ada put her head round the door of the sitting-room where they were quietly reading in front of the fire, and said that Mr Gilchrist had asked if they'd pop in to see him on their way to bed.

'Have you got that key safe?' were his first words as they put their heads round the door. They replied that they had. Malcolm had hung it round his neck as requested, in a little wash-leather bag suspended by a thin cord. 'I should wrap it in something else as well,' the old man said. 'Polythene or something of that sort — something non-conductive and protective. Put it under your pillow when you go to bed.' He cleared his throat. 'I thought I should tell you what conclusions I have come to.'

The boys waited attentively. Simon had perched himself on the foot of the bed, Malcolm sitting in a rather uncomfortable Victorian balloon-backed chair.

'I believe,' their great-uncle said, weighing his words carefully, 'that the key is a kind of talisman. When Mrs Clarke said I was only to use it in a time of great danger, I believe she thought that at some time — maybe in the distant future — the Forces of Evil, for that is what the Captain and his friends are, make no mistake, would try to reach her through me. They desperately need to get hold of the substance — whatever it is — and she is the only person who knows where it is hidden.'

'And they suspect that she may have told you something, some clue, at your last meeting? Anyway, what about Grandma — wasn't she in danger too?'

'Not as much. I think Mrs Clarke realised that your grandmother would try to put the whole affair out of her mind — pretend it had never happened or make up some explanation for it. That's why I never told her what Mrs Clarke had said that afternoon at Lady Tullich's. And I made her swear not to mention anything else to anybody. I told her that it was her fault the box had been opened in the first place, and that was what had alerted the Captain, and put Mrs C's life in danger. I think she felt quite bad about it — anyway I know she was happy to pretend it had never happened, and in a while she seemed to believe it too. I was never very close to her after that time.' He sighed.

'That's why I was so hurt when I heard your grandmother's story about seeing Mrs Clarke that time in 1944. All that time, working, slaving away trying to find a solution year after year, experimenting for *her* sake and wasting my life in the process. And yet she alights, as easy as the first swallow in the spring, in Lucy's garden. Probably gives one look into the window, sees there's nothing for her there, with those giggling, galumphing girls; sorry boys, I know I'm talking about your mothers, but it's the truth. So, without contacting me, off she goes again.'

'Wait a minute,' Simon said. He was frowning. 'I think I've got some idea why . . . listen, what factors were present in 1917, in 1944 and now? There was a war on the first two times, but not now — the first time was in the Christmas holidays, and so is this, but in 1944 Grandma said distinctly that it was early spring. There's something else — you and Gran? — No, that's not right — I've got it — children!'

'Children?' echoed Malcolm faintly.

'Yes, yes — don't you see — first of all it was Uncle Henry and Lucy, I mean Grandma, now it's us, but in 1944 it was Cathy and Liz — our mothers. Mrs C must have taken one look at them and realised that they wouldn't do. And Uncle Henry didn't have any — so there wasn't any point contacting him.'

They fell silent. Tension twanged the air; something, some intangible something embraced them with a feeling of expectancy, of warning.

'Simon!' Malcolm had been standing at the window, holding the curtain slightly drawn back. His cousin jumped off the bed, ran over to him.

'Down there, by the gate. Shut your eyes and open them quickly — now!' For an instant both saw the waiting figure. Then the wind, gusting, rattled the branches of the fir trees, obscuring their vision. When it had subsided, there was nothing.

The boys turned back to the bed. Uncle Henry's hands were clenched on his sheet. He looked old, ill. 'Was it him?'

'Yes,' Malcolm said. Simon, more cautious, stayed silent.

'There's one other thing I want you to see. Go to the desk and get out a brown envelope which you will find in the little top right-hand drawer. It's marked "Map".'

It was found, and brought to him; a tracing paper document which had been drawn out in pencil, then inked over. 'Copied it in the British Museum, years ago, they won't let you take it out of the map room y'know. Edinburgh, Old Town, 1793. Now look! Look closely. The part from the Castle down to Holyrood. All these narrow wynds and closes. Marked by numbers — see, the key's down below. Look on the right, going down. Niddry Street, first, that's still there, Dickson's Close, Caul's Court — all gone now. Now, see this opening — how it widens out, not like the others. Number 13 on the plan. Strickens C.C. That means Close. Note that. And what comes next, eh, going East? Blackfriars Wynd, which is now Blackfriars Street. Where Lucy and I came out that night. There *was* a court there. That's where the trail begins.'

'And what's there now?' Malcolm asked.

'You saw it — all demolished. They're going to put up office blocks, I shouldn't wonder.' He leaned back, his burst of energy gone.

'Uncle Henry,' Simon said in a coaxing voice, 'you haven't told us what your conclusions are. About the key and everything.'

'Well, say your theories about the substance being hidden somewhere in the future, only to be released by some pre-set combination of time and circumstances, are correct. Then the chances are that the Captain, if it is him you saw, is hanging about to catch Mrs Clarke when she returns here — as he believes she must. And the key has some power by which we can call her to our help, if we need it.'

'So we must try to elude the Captain, put him on a wrong scent, and then try and contact her, using the key?'

'Yes, or she may well contact you first. It's all so confusing. I think you should go to bed now. It's very late, and I'm tired.'

They told him their plans for visiting the Old Town and the Museum tomorrow.

'Do what you like, *but be on your guard*. Take Bina out to tea. There's money in my wallet — in the pocket of that coat behind the door. Take five pounds. And don't follow the Captain whatever you do.' His voice trailed away.

'Thank you, Uncle, it's very generous of you.'

Closing the door quietly behind them, they left the room.

CHAPTER NINE

It was the following afternoon; the three of them, Bina, Simon and Malcolm, stood at the foot of the Castlegate, about to cross over into the Lawnmarket.

'Across the road here,' Bina said in the tones of a guide, 'was the old West Bow. It housed a wicked warlock — maybe a relation of your Captain. He supped with the Devil, and every night he was called for by a black coach pulled by headless horses. He had a stick which went out on its own and did his bidding. After his death, his house was so badly haunted by ghouls and ghosties that it had to be pulled down.'

'Sounds like a great place for a horror film. Perhaps it reappears on Hallowe'en, creaking and groaning, with Vincent Price leaning out of an upstairs window . . .'

'Don't be daft,' called Bina over her shoulder as they crossed the road. 'Anyway, the West Bow doesn't exist any more, except for a wee bit down near the Grassmarket.' They hurried along. 'Now here is where the Jekyll and Hyde character, Deacon Brodie, lived. This was his house.'

'It looks pretty grim. What did he do?'

'He was a magistrate by day and a cut-throat by night. It's all in a book I have out from the library — you can read it yourselves.'

They spat for luck into the stone heart of Midlothian where the Tolbooth Jail once stood; and she gave them a running commentary on St Giles, and a glimpse inside, with a short history of the Luckenbooths. They came to the Tron and crossed over the Bridges. Now they were on the ground covered by those two other children in 1917. The traffic roared by as they dodged across Niddry Street. Boarded hoardings concealed the waste ground where building was in progress on the site of the old wynds, and the magic Stricken's Close. Then, Blackfriars Street. But it was all changed — there was nothing left of the door onto the pavement behind which two new half-crowns had rested on a ruined step. They paused. Twilight hung smokily in the cold air.

'It's no good, even with the map,' Malcolm said. 'It's all been destroyed.' He sounded dejected.

'Let's go and have tea,' Bina suggested. 'We can do the Museum and the Library another day.'

The restuarant was rather grand. It had recently been redecorated to look Victorian, with potted plants and red velvet seats. The waiters looked superciliously at the two boys in their jeans and anoraks. Bina, however, tall for her age and looking rather elegant in a long brown cloak and scarf, with her scarlet boots, seemed to meet with their approval. She inclined her head graciously as they were brought extra hot water.

'What a price for afternoon tea!' she exclaimed as she smashed a meringue. 'Hardly worth it — nothing home-made.'

Malcolm felt uncomfortable. He glanced at Simon, who seemed to be unaware of his surroundings, his mouth full of buttered toast.

'Well,' Bina remarked, filling the teapot. 'So you still stick to your story of seeing the Captain?'

'I know *I* did,' Malcolm said. 'Simon seems to be having second thoughts.'

'Not true. I know I saw someone that night I looked out of the landing window, but I suppose it could have been a burglar or — or something,' he ended rather lamely. 'I'm not sure about last night, or even that time coming back from the supermarket. There could have been explanations for both of those.'

'You were pretty scared when you came upstairs after you thought you'd seen him the first time. I thought you were going to cry!'

'Boys, boys!' Bina broke in. 'Will you stop quarrelling? There's no point to it. For myself, I must beg to remain sceptical.' She removed the cake plate from Malcolm and placed it on the stand. 'You are overweight already; it is very dangerous at your age.'

'I'd like to try out that key,' murmured Simon, closing his eyes in the smoky atmosphere.

'It didn't work yesterday, when I had a wish,' Bina said, drinking the last of her tea.

'Could have been because you didn't wish hard enough, like Uncle Henry when he was trying to get the stuff back into the box. Anyway, if the Captain *is* hanging around — OK, Mal, let's assume I believe it for the time being — then we ought to draw him away somehow before we go calling Mrs Clarke up.'

Bina shuddered. 'You make it sound like black magic. I think we ought to go. There's such a noise in here that I can hardly hear what you're saying, and it's so smoky — I feel faint.' She leaned back, pale and listless.

'Bina! Are you all right?' Malcolm asked anxiously.

She waved a long, lily hand. 'Order the Rolls for seven-thirty and tell my maid I'll be wearing the silver lamé and my black velvet cloak with the fox fur collar.' Abruptly, she stood up and looked around for their waiter. 'I expect the Captain or his spies have been here all the time, listening to our conversation. They've probably bugged that potted palm. Oh, let's get out of here — I want to finish my library book. It's far more exciting than anything you've told me.' She sounded sharp, strained. The boys paid the bill, adding some money of their own.

When they were waiting for a bus in Princes Street, Malcolm said: 'What do you think of Simon's theory — you know, that there had to be children present to complete the special set of circumstances under which the substance was to be released?'

'*Children?*' was Bina's only rejoinder. 'My dear Malcolm, you and Simon may think of yourselves as children, but I can assure you that *I* am not!'

She swept onto the bus with dignity and refused to say another word. When they parted at her gate, however, she promised to come over after supper and lend them the book she was reading, on condition they let her have it back the next day, when it was due to be returned to the library.

Their uncle was much better and wanted to hear all about their afternoon. When they told him that, in spite of their search, they had not been able to discover the slightest trace of Stricken's Close, he shook his head.

'I didn't think you would — I've been over that ground more than once myself. So that's a cold trail. Maybe it's a warning not to meddle further. I've been thinking things over today, while you were out. I don't want to feel that I've got you lads into any kind of danger. Maybe it would be best to forget all about it. I feel better today, much stronger, and that visit from Lucy, your grand-mother, cheered me up a lot — something I suppose I've got you two to thank for. I think she could be right — it's high time to put all that nonsense behind me. Give me back the key and I'll lock it up again in the desk — maybe even throw it away.'

Simon exchanged a glance with his cousin.

'Let me hang on to it just for this evening, sir. That pattern on it is very interesting and I wanted to copy it out for Ma — you know she's been doing a course in jewellery recently and I thought she might like to use it on a bracelet or something.'

Uncle Henry shot him a glance from under bushy brows. Simon returned his gaze innocently.

'Well, just for tonight. I want it back tomorrow morning. And now I can hear Ada calling you. I think she's got a little treat for your supper.'

The 'little treat' turned out to be Ada's idea of hamburgers, very overdone and crumbly, and served with a rather runny cauliflower cheese. They appreciated her effort, however, and managed to eat most of it, even offering to help her with the washing-up. Bina had arrived with the book just as they were finishing this task and was persuaded to come up and say goodnight to Uncle Henry. The boys rather hoped that she might sweet-talk the old man into letting them hang on to the key a bit longer, but she was not in the mood to bring that subject up.

It was while the three of them were standing at the door, making their goodbyes, that they heard it. An unmistakable, rusty jangling, coming from the kitchen passage. They rushed to the banister and looked down as Ada hobbled through the kitchen door. The clatter continued, growing more insistent.

'It's thae bells again,' she moaned. 'I'm not answering — I tellt ye before.'

Heaving himself into his dressing-gown, Uncle Henry appeared behind them. 'Stay here,' he ordered. 'You'll do no good . . .'

But they were already halfway down the stairs, Bina a pace or two behind the boys. 'Have you got the key?' she called. In answer, Malcolm held it up. Catching up, she slipped her hand into Simon's. As they reached the front door, the bells stopped as suddenly as they had begun. In the silence that followed, Malcolm slowly unbolted and opened the door.

There was nobody outside.

Cautiously, they stepped out. It was very cold and a few stray flakes of snow fluttered down. No one hiding in the front garden, even in the darkness of the laurel bushes. At the gate they paused and looked up and down the road. They did not feel frightened, but everything about them seemed to have taken on a dreamlike quality.

From the house behind them they could hear Uncle Henry calling 'Come back, come inside!' but his voice seemed to fade into the distance. They were conscious of a low-pitched humming, like a dynamo gathering strength. It died away.

They were still in the avenue. A man with a long pole was walking up the dark road. He thrust the pole through the bottom of each lamp glass, and pale gaslight flowered about them. A little further down the road, on the same side, a car was waiting, drawn up by the kerb.

It was a vintage Rolls Royce, high in the chassis, with brass side lamps. A chauffeur in uniform sat at the wheel. When he saw them, he got down from his seat and came round to the passenger door, which he held open.

'Well, what are we waiting for?' enquired Bina, mounting inside without hesitation. The boys followed. A fur rug was placed over their knees, the door was closed and the chauffeur took his place at the wheel once more. Slowly he turned about and they began to move downhill. Bina started to laugh.

CHAPTER TEN

They turned left at the Roseburn. Bina dropped the rug which she had been cuddling to her chin.

'This is luxury,' she sighed. 'Long may it continue.'

Simon, who had been craning out of the window, turned and looked at her. 'Bina! Your dress!'

It was glittering in the passing lamplight. Silver. Round her neck was a silver fox-fur collar, attached to a black velvet cloak. Her eyes shone.

'All I need is my tiara.'

'You forgot to ask for it.'

'So I did.'

'Look at that! Trams! Cable cars!'

'And cabs — four-wheelers! We've done it, Si! Gone back to . . . when?'

'Nineteen-seventeen I should think.'

'Just look at that model T Ford! And all those people — what clothes they're wearing! Look, over there — those soldiers in First World War uniforms. I can't see very well, the lighting is so dim and blue.'

They fell over one another to look, first from one side, then another. 'Look out!' cried Bina. 'You're ruining my dress.' Then she forgot. 'Princes Street! It can't be — it's so *different*!'

'Si, look — steam engines down on the railway, see them?'

'Oh, do sit still for a minute – you'll have the whole thing over. We're going up the Mound now – to the High Street, I should think!'

The car drew up at St Giles Cathedral. Solemnly, the chauffeur opened the door and handed Bina out. The boys followed.

'Whose car is this, then?'

There was no reply. The man remounted and the car drew away, back in the direction of the Castle. Now they were on their own and, as though to emphasise this, Bina was back in her ordinary clothes.

'What a bore!' she complained. 'And now what are we supposed to do? Have a ride in a cable car? I know, I shall hire a four-wheeler cab and go shopping down in Princes Street.'

'Don't be an idiot, you haven't any money for one thing. Anyway, I don't think we're meant to fool about here. That was just the first stage of the journey. It's as though something keeps telling me we'll have to go back to when Uncle and Grandma . . .'

'Here, hold hands,' interrupted Simon. 'That humming's begun again. What year should we think ourselves back to?'

'Oh, the end of the eighteenth century. When was it Uncle said? Seventeen ninety-eight, I think. Or thereabouts.'

The humming was stronger. They joined hands. In chorus they chanted: 'Seventeen-ninety-eight . . . seventeen-ninety-eight . . . seventeen —'

The street was growing misty, fading before their eyes, taking with it the vintage cars, the horse-drawn cabs, the dim blue of gas lighting. The humming rose to a crescendo, then died to nothing.

'Open your eyes!' ordered Simon, on a note of alarm. They looked around.

The tall, swag-bellied houses teetered above them, their false fronts of wood seeming to rock in the keen wind. It was daylight, somewhere high above them lay a cold, grey sky. An open drain ran down the middle of the narrow street; the smell was over-powering. Crowds jostled them, women shawled in faded plaids, barefoot boys, here and there the scarlet coat of a soldier.

'Ugh, the stink! I shall be sick!' cried Bina.

A pig ran past her, after it a barefooted woman brandishing a stick and shouting. On the far side of the street, two young men were quarrelling. One drew a sword, the other fell across the drain. A crowd gathered. Suddenly, the children were afraid.

'I hate it,' Bina shivered. 'Let's get out now! Quickly! Get the key and . . .'

'Shut up, and concentrate!' Malcolm ordered, although he felt his legs trembling. 'We've been sent back here for some good reason. I think, for a start, we should try to find the shop in Stricken's Close. Look at the street names, if you can see them, and count the openings. I think we're invisible, more or less, but keep to the wall and try not to attract attention.'

'It's getting so dark — oh here's Niddry Street.'

'Remember the map; this one's got no name, but it must be Dickson's Close. Two more; Caul's court; can't see the name on this one — Here! Stricken's Close! Down this way, quick!'

They dived into the narrow opening. There was a short passage, then it widened into the courtyard, just as their uncle had described. No lights or music this time; the place was, apparently, deserted. They ran towards the shop, lying across the court to the left, with its dusty bow window shuttered.

They mounted the steps and pushed at the door, which was, unexpectedly, unlocked. Faint light streamed in with them. The doorbell jangled faintly, but nobody came. The interior was bare — on the floor one dirty white silk stocking; on the counter a faded card, and on it, in flowing writing:

Orra Things Bought and Sold

Bina drifted round the counter. Her bright eyes spied one or two escaped trinkets, which she put in her pocket. Then she called to the boys.

'Look at this!'

She held out a folded, dusty paper, sealed with brown wax, and addressed, in the same hand, in blackish ink:

To Mistress Clarke

'Bina, you mustn't open that!'

'If Mistress Clarke hasn't come for her letter in nearly two hundred years, she won't be coming now,' Bina said tartly as she broke the seal.

'But we've *gone back* two hundred years in time. She could still be coming for it! You're like Grannie and the box. Typical girl!'

Simon reached for the paper. 'Oh shut up, Mal! It's done now, let's have a look at it.'

He carried it to the door where, peering over one another's shoulders, in the dim light they made out:

> *If so be that I am taken captive by those whom we ken weel (and I am in hourly dread and expectation of this end), then, if ye canna mak speed yer ain sel, send yr. accredited messengers with all haste tae the White Friars at the sign of the Sun in Cowgate, and pray God for my soul . . . Demosthenes.*

They refolded the paper. Simon replaced it reverently beneath the counter, well hidden this time.

'Accredited messengers?'

'I'm not sure. He may have meant Uncle and Gran, but I think the message is for us, now. That's why we've been brought here.'

'Wonder why it wasn't found before, when they ransacked the place.'

'He may have managed to get someone to bring it back here, after his capture. Well, we're too late to do anything for the poor old man now. So we had better do as he says — go to this place in the Cowgate. Come on!'

They gave a last, hurried look around — nothing else was to be found. Down the steps and out into the court, pulling the door behind them. They paused for a second before entering the crowded High Street.

'We must keep together, touching if possible. On no account must we be separated. Mal — you go first, with the key. Hold tight on to it.'

'Ugh, a rat!' Bina screamed, clinging to Simon. 'Oh, these ghastly people, they look like murderers, all of them!'

79

'Don't shout, Bina — you might be noticed. Follow me — we'll go down Niddry Street.'

But Bina pulled back. 'I'm not going down the Cowgate for anyone. It looks like the mouth of hell! You know the plague was there — probably still is for all we know! It was all in that book I was reading. They sealed up the houses with the dead inside them.' She was weeping hysterically.

Malcolm put his arm round her. 'Don't worry, you'll be safe with us. We'll take care of you.' He sounded more courageous than he felt. Bina produced a handkerchief, blew her nose.

'I loathe the eighteenth century — there's nothing romantic about it.' She seemed to pull herself together. Down, down into the musty dark they went, past dimly lit drinking shops where brawls were mounting, past drunkards reeling and spinning, past caddies with their water cans strapped to their backs.

Nobody noticed them. It was as if they were invisible. Bina, recovering, even started to chatter. 'Imagine carrying water up all those stairs! And, at a certain hour of the day, you know, the people emptied their slops out of the top windows, calling Gardy Loo, which meant *garde l'eau*, that's French, you know, for . . .'

'We seem to have heard all this somewhere before, haven't we, Mal?' Simon enquired. They had now reached the lowest level. They had come into the Cowgate, that low, dark thoroughfare which runs under the Bridges from east to west, but which was, at that time in its history, a great deal more dark, unsavoury and evil. Bina stopped, leaned against Malcolm.

'I can't — I can't breathe here — I'm sorry — I — I can't go any further,' she gasped. The two boys looked at her. She was very pale. As they watched, she closed her eyes and seemed to sag. They caught her, each holding one of her arms. They looked around them.

A fog was rolling to meet them. Not only did it obscure all before them, it was as thick as porridge, sticky as liquid rubber. Try as they would, it blocked them, kept them standing, closed round them.

'Behind you — look out!' Malcolm shouted.

Simon turned. He saw Malcolm's nightmare come to life. Saw gigantic chimney figures, moving easily. Stone monoliths, with smoking hair, pressing forward towards them, wreathed in tendrils of fog. Their feet stuck to the ground and they were unable to move, to escape. Beneath them the earth shook to the thump of the giants. Bina slid to the dirty cobbles, her hands clutching Malcolm's knees. His mouth was dry, his fingers shaking, but he knew what to do.

He took out the key, held it up in front of him.

It began to glow, first dimly, then with a rapidly increasing radiance which soon enclosed all three of them. Into that clear and glowing circle of light no fumes or fog could penetrate, no evil come.

The stones, the chimney men, fell back and the wisping tentacles of fog retreated with them. Slowly, the children moved forward, the two boys supporting Bina between them. As they advanced, the circle of light moved with them. Gradually, they gained in confidence.

They found themselves standing before a building with an arched, oaken door, rather like a church door. Above it hung a gilded sign, a sun surrounded by wavy, stylised rays.

'This must be it. The sign of the Sun in Cowgate.'

Simon knocked three times.

Footsteps sounded down a stone-flagged passage within. A small flap in the door slid back, a boy's face looked through a grille.

'Who sent you?'

'Demosthenes,' Simon said firmly.

'The sign?'

Malcolm held up the key. The door bolts were drawn back, the heavy door swung open, and they were beckoned inside. The boy, in a monk's white habit, locked and bolted the door behind them. Indicating that they were to follow him, he led them through a passage, then an open cloister, and up a spiral stone stair. As they climbed they heard a pounding at the door by which they had entered. The pounding came like the beats of a heart, a heart of stone. Doom! Doom! Doom!

Surely no door could withstand that battering?

Then, from the chamber at the head of the staircase, there came a sound. A word. It hummed out like a million bees, growing in volume, encompassing the building, the children, all within. It was a hum a thousand times deeper, stronger, more powerful than the hum they heard with the key.

Three times it came, whilst they paused outside the chamber door.

The pounding stopped and there was complete silence.

The boy in the white monk's habit knocked on the door to the chamber. They heard no voice from inside, but he opened it and gestured for them to go in. The door was shut behind them.

They were in a spherically shaped room, with a high, vaulted roof, lit from an unseen source. A circular table, with a highly polished surface like white marble, stood in the centre. Around it, seated on massive, high-backed oaken chair, were twelve men. From what the children could see of them, they were clothed in chainmail, with long white tabards over it. On the front of each tabard was a red cross, its design curiously echoing that of the key which Malcolm still held — a cross within a circle. Their heads were bare, each circled with a narrow band of silver. Opposite the children, at the far side of the table, and seated slightly back from it, was a man, dressed also in the white tabard with its red cross, but with a long purple cloak flung back from his shoulders, and a chaplet of gold on his brown hair.

In the midst of the table they saw a globe of crystal, and in the globe a point of intense light. They stood, waiting, uncertain of what to do. The man facing them spoke.

'So, my children, you come from Demosthenes.' The voice was deep, gentle.

'Actually, no, sir. You see, we read this letter, and . . .'

'It had been left behind, you see, and we thought . . .'

'Mistress Clarke,' Bina found her voice, which sounded faint and high.

'Ah, yes. I know whom you mean.' A smile irradiated his face.

'Show me the sign.'

Malcolm held out the key. It had ceased to glow, but had a silver sheen. A great silence held the hall.

'Do you know why you are come here?'

'We had to come.'

'True, Malcolm, you have been chosen. Yet, you still have a choice, to go on — or to turn back now.'

'We must go on.'

'And the others?'

Simon nodded; Bina made no motion.

'There will be great danger, but you are protected.'

'By the key?'

'Truly by the key; yet not by that alone.'

Simon spoke; awkwardness roughened his voice. 'What do you want us to do?'

'Take up the key, and touch the crystal. Don't be afraid.'

'I can't reach it!'

Yet the key seemed to grow, to stretch over the table until its light touched the point of light in the crystal ball. All clouded into fire and smoke, and when this cleared they saw a great company of Knights, all in full armour now, and with the red crosses clearly marked on their breasts, marching through a mountainous landscape. At their head a man rode on a great white horse; they could not see his face, but around his helmet was a chaplet of gold. Below him and a little to one side a woman rode, wrapped in a blue cloak. Her face could not be seen. And behind them, another figure, a boy dressed like a page. He carried in front of him, on the pommel of his saddle, an object wrapped in a shiny, golden material.

As they watched this procession winding its way amongst the rocks, there came a roll of thunder and the sky darkened. From a deep canyon in the mountain ahead of them appeared another army. Black-armoured knights mounted on black horses, with billowing banners like thunderclouds in the livid light. As it advanced, Bina closed her eyes. She could hear the clang of steel, the screaming horses, almost smell the blood upon the ground. When she opened them again, it was to a scene of devastation. The page boy lay dying, and the woman in the blue cloak was bending above him. She picked up the gold-wrapped casket and rode swiftly away with it. For a while she was unnoticed, then a black-visored knight wheeled his horse and rode in pursuit. As she fled, his great black charger reared, vast wings spread like a bat, and a dragon fire breathed from its nostrils. It flew into the air, and behind them, in a dreadful train, rode the black armies, charred paper against a burning sky.

A mist rose, covering the woman.

The scene faded.

'Was that Mrs Clarke?' Malcolm cried. 'What happened then? Was that the casket she was carrying?'

The Knight-King (for somehow they knew he was a king) answered:

'Many hundreds of years have passed since that battle. You saw but one affray in a struggle which has lasted since the creation of the world. And must go on until there is balance between light and dark, good and evil.'

'Why did you show it to us? What are we meant to do?'

'You can do a great deal, my children. We will guide you. On you may depend the success of the plan laid by the one you call — Mistress Clarke. You must recover the Martlet Casket.'

Suddenly Bina spoke out. 'I think Mrs Clarke is a bore and a nuisance. I don't want anything more to do with this. It's gone on long enough!'

'Alas, my child, I fear it is too late!' Once more the King directed them to look into the crystal. 'You will now be shown the casket. Only you will be able to see it, and that for a brief space of time, so mark closely all that you can tell about it.'

The mist swirled. Again it cleared.

84

The casket appeared for the first time to their eyes, but dimly, as though seen through dusty glass. Resting on a piece of dusty green — velvet? baize? Impossible to tell.

It receded from them faster and faster, the chamber and the knights in it grew smaller and smaller, like dolls around a cotton reel. A voice cried: 'Take hands — hold the key.'

And then someone was calling their names. It was their uncle. 'All right, Simon? Malcolm? Bina? Come back to me, all of you.' Light began to grow once more.

They were all back in the study at number twelve, kneeling rather foolishly on the hearthrug, and Uncle Henry was bending over them, chafing Bina's hands with a worried look.

CHAPTER ELEVEN

'Exactly what happened to us, as you saw it?' Simon asked his great-uncle. He was drinking tea with both hands round the cup for warmth.

'I called you — you were standing in the road, staring at nothing.'

'Not nothing, Uncle Henry, a vintage Rolls.'

'I didn't see anything. As far as I was concerned, the road was empty. I called you to come in —'

'Yes, we heard you.'

'— and you turned, like automata, and came. You walked past me into this house, into this room, and sat down, round the table, staring with your eyes open. I spoke to you several times, but you said nothing. Nothing! And then I realised something of what was happening . . . Help yourself to more tea, Bina . . . I seemed to be told to sit down with you, make you hold hands, and hold your hands, so that we formed a circle. I sat like that with you for over half an hour, not moving, not talking. Until, quite suddenly, first one, then another, then all three of you slipped down off your chairs onto the floor, and I knew I could call you back.'

'Didn't you hear anything?'

'I thought once there was a sort of humming sound, like a dynamo, but I may have been mistaken.'

'Did we speak?'

'Now and again Bina twitched, but no, none of you spoke.'

They looked at each other, feeling half in, half out of the world.

Their uncle, still in his dressing-gown, had somewhere found a biro and some sheets of exercise paper. These he put on the table.

'Now if you could just tell me . . .'

'Oh, no, not now! We couldn't.'

'You must, Malcolm, don't you see it's absolutely necessary to write it down before the details fade from your mind, like a dream.'

'It was a dream — or a nightmare, rather.' Bina drank her tea thirstily. 'A horrible nightmare. I want to forget it as soon as possible, in fact I *am* forgetting it. I don't want to talk about it.'

'What about you, Simon?'

Simon pushed up his glasses, rubbed his eyes. 'Could have been a hallucination,' he said sleepily. He pushed his hand through his dark, curly hair, making it stand on end. 'Perhaps it was something Ada put in those hamburgers. It *was* vivid, though — almost real. I wonder if there really is some power in the key — perhaps contained in the metal . . .'

'It wasn't a dream, or a hallucination,' Malcolm interrupted. 'Put your hand in your pocket, Bina, and show us what you have there.'

She put her long fingers gingerly down and drew out three rusty objects. A shoe buckle, a thimble, a ring.

'Well?'

Bina turned pale and was silent. She left the objects on the table and took no further notice of them.

'Interesting! Hmmm. Hmmm!' Uncle Henry tried to speak calmly, but his hand trembled as he took up the buckle. 'Just like Lucy's trinkets.' He poised the pen once more, turning to Simon. 'Tell me slowly, in your own words.'

Haltingly, reluctantly, Simon began. Gradually, as the story unfolded he became more confident, and Malcolm joined in, corroborating and correcting. Yet, when it came to the story of the house in the Cowgate, and their meeting with the Knights, Bina spoke for the first time.

'I don't remember any of that.'

'You *must*, Bina. You were there.'

'Well, I'm telling you I don't! I remember running down that dark wynd — Niddry Street, I think it was, and a sort of horrible fog, and not being able to breathe. And that's all!'

Malcolm turned red. 'But you spoke! To the King, or whatever he was — the chief Knight. You *must* remember!'

'What King? What Knights? I don't know what you're on about. All this has made me feel ill. What's the point in writing it all down. It's horrible.'

Their uncle closed the book. 'Perhaps Bina is right. After all, you're under age, you're my responsibility. I shouldn't let you go on with it. You're just children.'

'Just children? I thought that was the whole point of the exercise.'

'Listen, Simon. I failed — that's my affair, but I'm not letting you three get into mortal danger, even for *her* sake.'

'What about the world then? According to the Knights, it's in mortal danger.'

'We'll be protected,' pleaded Malcolm. 'The Knight-King told us. And we've got the key. They wanted us to go on — that's why they gave us the clue about the casket — where it was hidden. They need us to find it so that they can lock the substance up in it again, once it's been released from its hiding place.'

'What clue?' Uncle Henry, despite his misgivings, was interested.

'We didn't see it very well — it was behind glass, I think, on a sort of green velvet. I don't know why, but I got the feeling it wasn't too far away.'

'It could have been in a cabinet of some kind — an old-fashioned china cabinet, perhaps, like the one in the drawing-room here. That has a green baize on its shelves, I think — most of them did. Could it have been something like that?'

Malcolm nodded. 'Now I come to think of it, I'm sure I remember a polished wooden strut, like you find on cabinet doors when they are divided into glass panels. I'm sure it was something like that. But there must be hundreds of houses with old-fashioned china cabinets in Edinburgh. We don't even know where to start.'

Bina picked up the *Evening Express* and hid behind it, to show she had no further interest in the conversation. Malcolm was irritated.

'It's easy for you to be sarky and do nothing,' he said heatedly.

'Leave her alone.' Simon sounded tired. 'If she doesn't want to have anything to do with — with what's happened, that's her lookout. I almost wish . . .'

From the direction of the French windows came a peremptory tapping on the glass. There was silence.

The rapping came again. Even Bina laid down her paper.

Uncle Henry crossed the room. He pulled back the heavy curtains. Then, without hesitation, he unbolted the window.

A lady entered.

She wore a long fur cloak with an upturned collar. On her head was a tall fur hat; she carried a muff with long tails hanging down. She was beautiful, but extremely pale. Her eyes were unnaturally large and, in this light, dark.

'Lalla!' croaked Uncle Henry. He seemed to break into tears. 'After all those years, you have come back at last!'

'Yes, Harry, I have come back.' The voice was brisk, rather husky, with a slight foreign intonation. 'Draw the curtain and bolt the window, Malcolm. You can take my coat, Simon, and shake it well — it is snowing again. And wake up, all of you. There is work to be done!'

Everyone except Bina moved in a flurry of activity — bolting the window, shaking her cloak (which she now removed), offering her a chair by the fire. She was dressed in a suit of dark, chrysanthemum red velvet, its cut very similar to those they had seen earlier as they drove along Princes Street in the year 1917 — a long flaring tunic-coat over a narrow, ankle-length skirt. The fur hat was taken off, to reveal flaming red-gold hair, swept to the crown of her head in an elaborate whirl.

'So, my poor Harry, life hasn't treated you well, has it?' She held out her hand and the old man knelt, weeping openly now, at her knee, to the shame and embarrassment of his nephews. 'Dry your tears, you must not fail me this time.'

But Uncle Henry was not so easily consoled. 'All these years! Never a word, never a message.'

'Has it really been so long? I am sorry, but time goes so quickly for us. Your whole mind was clouded with thoughts of failure and depression — that's why I could not reach you. But now is the time for success!' She turned to smile at them all. She flamed, she was lit with the smile. He rose, creaking slightly, from his rheumaticky knees. He sniffed and blew his nose.

'Thought you must have forgotten me — I was beginning to think I'd never see you again.'

'Well, Harry, now you see you were wrong. There is a time for everything. One has to wait for the acceptable time.' She crossed her ankles in boots with light kid uppers — her smile for the old man was compassionate, but amused.

Then she turned to the three children. 'I may be a stranger to you, but in reality I know you quite well. Of course, you know who I am. Your uncle Henry and your grandmother knew me as Mrs Clarke, though your uncle has another name for me.' She smiled at him. 'I sent the car for you this afternoon. You did well on your travels. Your mothers, whom I once saw, were nice girls, but they had no *vision*. I was not quite sure of you, Simon, but I think you have learnt recently that there are "more things in heaven and earth than are dreamt of in your philosophy"? And you, child, no relation at all. Robina Henderson from next door. Well that could be all to the good.'

Bina spoke for the first time. 'Don't count me in, please, whatever it is you're planning. I don't want to have anything to do with it!'

'She was very scared this evening,' explained Malcolm.

'Scared? I wasn't scared. It was just a nightmare — a hallucination.'

'And the rusty trinkets?'

'Och, some rubbish I must have picked up somewhere and put in my pocket without thinking.'

'And Mrs Clarke?' prompted Malcolm.

'I don't know who she is,' sniffed Bina, 'but she's not a hundred years old — she's not even fifty. She just dressed up like that and came through the window to scare us for some reason. It's a practical joke.'

'I'm sorry you feel like that, Bina,' Mrs Clarke said gently. 'Would you like to go home now?'

Bina stood up and sank back. 'I feel giddy,' she cried.

Mrs Clarke took a small bottle from the recesses of her muff. 'Take my smelling salts. They will soon make you better.'

'I suppose this is a trick to put me in a trance again!'

'No, Bina, it is not. Try them and see.'

So Bina, fearfully, and reluctantly, took hold of the small, pink, cut-glass bottle, removed the stopper, and sniffed at it with caution. Gradually, as the others talked, she sat up, the colour coming back into her cheeks, and took notice.

'Mrs Clarke, there is one question I want to ask first.' This was Simon. 'Exactly how is time-travel done?'

'I thought you might ask me that, Simon, but I am afraid you must be patient. I can't answer you that at present.'

'How did you get here?' Malcolm wanted to know. 'And from where?'

'That's two questions. How? By the only safe way I know, through the back garden. And from where? Alas, another unanswerable question. But we must not waste time. The Captain is waiting — keeping watch outside this house — and I have not got very much time to spend here. So I want you children to concentrate, as hard as possible, on that vision you were given of the casket in its present resting place. Describe it, if you can.'

Malcolm again described the dim glass, the faded green background. He volunteered Uncle Henry's theory that it might be in a china cabinet somewhere.

'You did not see the room?'

Malcolm shook his head. Mrs Clarke put up her long, white fingers to her forehead and held them there, concentrating in thought. 'I think I am getting the picture,' she announced at last. 'I think I know where you must look. It is dangerous, however. We have to go back to a time when the Captain, as we call him, had a great deal of power. But I think your uncle has told you about him.'

She looked at their uncle. 'Have you told them everything?' He nodded.

'They — he and your grandmother — went back nearly a hundred and twenty years, time travelling. They came to the shop in Stricken's Close, where they found the old shopkeeper, Jamie Taggart, who was one of our chosen agents. He is also known as Demosthenes. He gave them the casket, but the Captain's men caught up with him. They tortured him, and in his agony he betrayed us.'

'You mean . . .?' breathed Uncle Henry.

'Yes, Harry. He admitted that you and Lucy were holding the casket in the year 1917. The Captain could not travel forwards in time, so he had to wait. He waited, for he knows that time lies in spirals, it has no spatial reality. Wait, Simon, I will discuss that with you some other time — let me finish my story now. The casket was sealed from harm until 1917. The Wise Knights, who you met tonight, arranged it. They are Lords and Masters of Time. But then Lucy and Harry tampered with the box instead of waiting until I came to claim it, which put them in great danger. I had to come and rescue them quickly, and take the casket before I was really ready. So the Captain and his friends were able to outwit me, and almost brought complete disaster.'

'But although you lost the casket,' interrupted Malcolm, 'you were able to protect the stuff that was in it, weren't you?'

Mrs Clarke was stern. 'Without the casket, the substance itself is vulnerable. I had to seal it with a magic formula — three times; in space, in time, in destiny. Space is discoverable, time is running out, and destiny is beyond my control.'

'Then what can we do?' asked Simon.

Bina caused an interruption by rising and crossing to Mrs Clarke.

'Thanks for the smelling salts,' she said. 'Goodnight.' She went to the door.

'You're not going now?' exclaimed Malcolm in astonishment.

'Goodnight,' repeated Bina, at the door.

'Goodnight, Bina,' said Mrs Clarke.

Bina went, without a backward glance, closing the door behind her.

'You ask what can be done,' Mrs Clarke continued. 'Destiny is against the Captain, because, although it is immortal and therefore beyond my control, he is on the side of evil, and evil by its very nature destroys itself in the end. Yet, if he has time on his side, he can delay destiny, and with it human progress. With time on his side he can conquer space. So time must not be wasted. We have too little of it and there is so much to be done.'

'So we were right — you have put a sort of time-switch mechanism on the substance, and when it goes off the little ball can be found.'

'More or less, Simon. And so I need your help, all of you.'

'Why us?'

The door opened, unobserved by all except Mrs Clarke, and Bina stole back into the room looking white as a peeled stick.

'Why you? Because you are not only young — and the young are open-minded on the whole — but because you boys are on a special vibration, related as you are to my dear Harry. What is the matter, Bina?'

'I can't go out the front door. There's someone there — watching the house. He frightened me.'

'Sit down, my dear, and in a minute I will see you safely home through the back garden.' Mrs Clarke turned to the boys. 'Are you willing to help me?'

'How I wish I were young again!' came from their great-uncle, with something less than the truth.

'Now, Harry, your job is to co-operate with me to protect the children.' She paused, consulting a small jewelled watch attached by a chain to her lapel. 'I must be going. I shall return tomorrow, Harry, at about the same time, to give you your instructions, and I should like your sister Lucy to be present.' She rose, held out her arms for her cloak. Malcolm sprang to help her before his uncle could move. Yet she crossed to the old man. 'My dear friend, dear Harry. Don't despair. We shall not fail this time.'

She kissed him gently on the cheek, and turned to take up her hat. 'Au revoir!' She put on her gloves and her muff. 'Come, Bina. You will be quite safe with me. You must never be afraid. Never run away from evil. Face it and it will dwindle and dwindle until it dissolves into nothing.' She looked very seriously into Bina's face, holding it by the chin, as though she saw something nobody else could see. Bina twisted out of her grasp. Now Mrs Clarke addressed them all, with her back to the curtained window.

'Don't come with me, any of you. We are safe. I am well protected this time, and you also are safe. I am ready now. Don't worry, Harry — you were always such a worrier!'

Uncle Henry stepped forward and kissed her gloved hand. Simon drew aside the curtain and unbolted the French windows. A flurry of cold air and a few snowflakes swept into the room.

'One last word. Keep the key well guarded. Now, pull the curtains behind me. I have a torch.' And, so saying, she drew it out of her muff and switched it on. In an instant she and Bina were out of the window; the curtain dropped into place behind them. Uncle Henry stumbled forward.

'I must see if she is all right.'

'I'll go, Uncle,' Malcolm volunteered. 'Where's your torch?'

'In the cupboard under the stairs, on a shelf. Put out the light before you draw the curtains.'

The torch was found and the room darkened. Malcolm opened the window and dashed out into the snow. Uncle Henry and Simon waited in silence for a few minutes. There were footsteps on the iron steps and Malcolm came back into the room, breathless and astonished.

'Well?'

'She — saw Bina to the gap in the hedge, waited until she went in through the back door of number thirteen. Then she just — vanished! It's true! One minute she was there, shining her torch for Bina — and the next she'd gone! No sign of her!'

'You missed her in the dark — it's snowing heavily now.'

'No, it's not — it's almost stopped. And I went down, into the garden. There were footprints — two lots. Bina's going away towards her house, and Mrs Clarke's, ending a few steps further on, right in the middle of the back lawn.'

They looked at one another, wondering.

CHAPTER TWELVE

Two days later, in the shadow of early evening, Malcolm and Simon stood in a dark alley between two towering tenements. They were in dockland Leith. Beyond the mouth of the close was the quayside, the dim bulk of ships at anchor. Mrs Clarke had given them their instructions, and they were about to enter the house which had once belonged to the Captain.

It was a derelict, crumbling ruin. Plastered across the front door they had seen a large notice:
DEMOLITION IN PROGRESS — DANGER — KEEP OUT.

'There is a side door in the alley which is unbolted,' she had told them. 'Make your way in, and up to the first floor. That is where you should find the casket. If danger threatens, hold up the key and call to me — *but not aloud, in your minds*. I will come to you. You must be on your guard at all times.'

It had begun to rain; a thin, sharp drizzle.

Malcolm produced his torch, but did not switch it on. Making sure that they were unobserved, they approached the door, turned the handle, and pushed. It opened easily. Drawing it to behind them, they entered and switched on the torch.

They were in a passage which led to a square hall. Out of the hall a stair went up, wide and formal, with oak banisters. On the newel posts were carved creatures, hooded like vultures, with lions' tails. The silence was watchful, waiting.

They climbed the stairs. Once a board groaned, tilting; silt and dust fell. There was a gap where a step was missing. They clung to the banisters then moved forward cautiously, testing each step and pausing to listen. When they reached the landing they looked around. On their left a door stood half open. The boys exchanged glances. Warily, they entered the room. From three long windows facing them a wan light filtered through grime onto bare floorboards. Two of the panes were broken and a loose slat hanging from the shutter rattled spasmodically in the wind.

'What was that?'

A rustle. A creak and a rumble which died away.

'In that corner! Look, Mal — look!'

The torch illuminated the far corner of the room. There, so broken and dilapidated that the builders had presumably not thought it worth the bother of removing, was a large, old-fashioned glass-fronted cabinet. Its door swung crazily, half wrenched off its hinges. It was empty.

'It *was* here, though.' Simon pointed to the middle shelf, where the worn green velvet showed a square of less faded material. 'It's been taken!'

Again came the rumble, louder this time. Loosened plaster fell in a thin rain from the battered moulding of the ceiling. The house, like a sleeping beast awakening, shook itself.

Fear twisted a knot round their hearts. A long second to look at each other, then they dashed for the door and through it, making for the stairs. Yet, even before they reached the topmost step, there was a roar like thunder, the banisters keeled over, the whole staircase seemed to drop away and they dropped with it, sliding ten feet or more to the half-landing. At the same time the ceiling above caved in, covering them in plaster. It was difficult to breathe, but worse than that was the fear, shutting out all else, paralysing and immobilising them. They sobbed, choking, scrabbling frantically in the dirt and dark, tearing their hands against lathes, panicking, waiting for the whole house to cave in finally and bury them.

It was Simon who recovered first.

'Stop it, Mal,' he gasped. 'Quiet! I thought I heard — a voice —'

They listened.

Then it came. Muffled but distinct. 'The key, Malcolm, take out the key.'

He was lying face downwards. With great difficulty, he moved one arm, pushed it inside his coat, encountered the cord and drew it up. At last he had the key in his hand.

The voice came again, stronger this time.

'Keep calm, and do exactly as I say.'

The key began to glow.

'Don't move suddenly. Be very, very cautious. Get up on your hands and knees. You will find you can move now. That's better. Now look down.'

They raised themselves slowly, and looked down into the hall, piled with debris. Beyond, faintly in the still-swirling dust, a light moved.

'I am down here. In a minute you will see me.'

'Mrs Clarke!'

She had appeared immediately below them, carrying a torch.

'You will have to jump. Don't be frightened — you will be perfectly all right. Hold up the key and I will give the word.'

Malcolm held up the key.

'Stand up. Now, Simon first — *jump*!'

Simon jumped. He fell the twelve feet into the stairwell, floating gently, reeling down into rubble.

'Jump, Malcolm!'

He launched himself after his cousin. It was like flying. No bother.

'Quick!' she ordered, taking their hands.

They seemed to skim across the tangle of boards and plaster, out into the fresh air, across the cobbled street to where their uncle waited for them in his car. As he held the door open, there was a noise like thunder. The Captain's house swayed, reached forward, dissolved in a roar and a cloud of dust. People came running, shouting.

They looked for Mrs Clarke, but she was nowhere to be seen.

* * *

A bright sunny morning in the avenue, and snow on the ground.

'There was a bit in *The Scotsman* this morning about that house falling down,' Bina shouted, running and kicking up the snow with her boots. 'You must have been mad to go in there, with "Danger" written on the door. It's a good thing nobody saw you.' She scooped up snow, threw it inexpertly at Simon and missed.

'Your grannie must have been daft to let you — of course your uncle isn't fit to be trusted.' She shrieked as a well-aimed snowball from Malcolm landed on the back of her neck. 'Stop it — that went down my neck.'

'Gran didn't know where we were going, neither did Uncle Henry. They were just told to stand by, in case.' Simon stopped running and leant against a tree. He was out of breath.

'You're out of condition, my lad,' Bina told him. 'It's all that rich foreign food. Very bad for your liver. Anyway, you didn't find what you were looking for, did you?'

'No, but we think we know where it is now.'

'*She* told you, did she?' Your wonderful Mrs Clarke? Pity she didn't tell you before, and save you a wild goose chase where you might have got yourselves killed.'

'I told you — it *was* in the Captain's house, but someone, and it's obvious who, had removed it. Anyway, she rescued us.'

Bina snorted derisively.

'I thought you were the one who saw him the other night, Bina,' Simon said quietly. 'It seemed to give you a bit of a shock at the time.'

'Och, that was just imagination — you got me so worked up I would have seen anything. Anyway, where *do* you think the casket is now?'

'Well, it's to do with a dream that Si had last night. Tell her what happened.'

Simon scraped a toe in the snow. 'I don't think she'd be very interested. After all, she thinks the whole thing is imagination — a product, no doubt, of my malfunctioning liver. Come on, Mal, let's go. We've got quite a lot of ground to cover this afternoon, remember.'

They had walked about twenty yards back towards their uncle's house when Bina caught up with them. She linked her arms with theirs.

'Suppose I said that I really *do* believe you — that I was just having you on before?'

The boys said nothing.

'Come on — don't be such spoil sports. I might be able to help you — I bet I know more about this city than you do.'

'All right,' Simon said eventually, 'but you're not to interrupt.' They had reached the gate of Bina's house.

'I couldn't sleep last night, just lay awake thinking about it all. I was trying to find some sort of — sensible answer. My eyes were fastened on a gap in the curtains where I could see a very bright star — Mars, Venus, I don't know. I must have drifted off, because there was this great beam of light in the room, like a laser, and it was drawing me up, into space, into the star. I don't know how to explain it, but I had the extraordinary feeling that the star *was* me — or I was the star, it doesn't matter which. Anyway, it felt marvellous, like being linked up to a huge power source. And suddenly I was awake again, but I could hear a voice saying, very clearly, "Try the Museum". That's all.'

'What sort of voice?'

'I don't know — just a voice. But I felt tremendously clear-headed after I woke up, as if I had got the answer to — not just my problem, but all the problems in the Universe.'

'Marvellous,' Bina said sharply. 'So on the strength of this brief commercial you're shooting off to some museum this afternoon to look for the magic casket?'

'I knew you wouldn't understand.'

Bina smiled suddenly. Her face lit up. 'Of *course* I understand, Simon dear. Which museum are you going to? I should try the Royal Scottish, in Chambers Street. I'd better come with you, to show you where it is. Meet you here, at two-thirty sharp.' She danced away up the path, blew them a kiss at the door. The boys stared after her.

'Crazy girl', Simon said. They went into lunch.

* * *

They took two buses to get to the Museum, because Bina said she could not walk up the Mound. They ascended the steps, crossed the wide hall with the fishpond, walked through several rooms, and stood watching the movement of the great pendulum which registers the pull of the earth. Then they moved off slowly towards the engineering exhibits.

'If it's of any interest to you,' Bina said languidly, 'I've just seen the Captain again. Have another piece of tablet?'

Malcolm helped himself to the fudge. 'Where?' he said.

'Behind that engine over there.'

The boys raced off, and she doubled up with laughter, leaning behind the case which housed a rotary pump.

They came back, black-looking.

'You're easy fooled. It's a crying shame,' she giggled.

A party of children in the charge of a teacher passed them.

Simon pressed a button on the rotary pump case. The pistons worked realistically. 'As I told you before, Bina, there's such a thing as crying "wolf" once too often. You may be sorry.'

She shrugged. 'I'm bored with all this machinery. Come on!' They drifted away, down a small corridor to the seismograph. They bent over the instrument, watching the steel needle suspended on the revolving drum, marking hours and minutes. It traced a straight, undeviating line across the chequered paper.

'Now, if it were to start trembling and shooting about — *he* might be in the offing!' Bina was overcome with hysterical giggles once more.

Simon looked at her. Behind his glasses his eyes were serious. 'I suggest we don't mention him out loud again. Or even think of him. Not on this excursion. I think he can read our thoughts, and

I also think you can give power to him by thinking about him. So let's try to keep our minds clear, OK?'

He turned to Malcolm.

'Have you got the key safe?'

'Yes.'

'Take it out of the bag and hold it. What does it feel like — is it hot, or cold?'

'What fun,' Bina sniffed. 'Like Hunt the Thimble.'

Simon looked at her and she fell silent.

'Come on,' Simon said, let's try upstairs. I don't think it's on this floor anyway.' They turned, made their way to the staircase. Bina hung back, showing interest in the goldfish swimming in the pool.

'What's up with her?' Malcolm whispered. 'She's been acting very oddly all day — I don't like it.'

Simon paused at the first stair. 'Nor do I; we'd better keep her close to us.' He yelled, 'Come on, Bina.'

She trailed towards them, wrapping her scarf around her mouth. 'Come on for what?' Suddenly, she ran up the stairs in front of them, looking over her shoulder down into the hall below. They followed.

'Key's definitely warmer now,' Malcolm murmured.

They turned left, down the main gallery, past glass cases full of ceramics, glancing casually at them as they went. Bina lagged behind once more, yet suddenly came running, clutching at Malcolm's arm.

'What's up now?'

'Nothing. What should there be? Look at that china shepherdess there, isn't she pretty? I expect she's Dresden. I'll have her when I marry my millionaire and go to live in my castle.'

Malcolm took a good look at the figurine. 'I think she's dreadul. Simpering like that in her silly hat, with a half-dead lamb lying at her feet. You can't be serious. What's up, Bina?'

Simon studied her, his head on one side.

'I'm afraid she thinks she's seen you-know-who for real this time.'

Bina let her head sink forward. Her long dark hair fell over her face. 'Of course,' came her voice from behind the curtain. 'What else could you expect? Let's go home now, please. I'm sick of museums.'

'The key!' Malcolm interrupted excitedly. 'It's burning hot — I can hardly hold it, even with my glove on!'

Simon looked round. 'Turn right!'

They clattered into a small gallery, devoted to old lace and historical costumes. From there they passed to a roped-off room arranged with eighteenth-century furniture. A uniformed attendant stood close by.

'It's scorching my fingers,' Malcolm whispered. 'It must be here. I wish that attendant would go.'

'Look — on that card-table!'

They stared. 'It looks like the casket.'

Across the passage stood trestles. A notice read:

> *These rooms are in the process of rearrangement;*
> *this gallery is closed to the public until further notice.*

They awaited in a fever of impatience. At last a woman came up to the attendant and asked a question — he moved away with her, not taking notice of the children.

'Now, quick!'

Simon vaulted the trestle, dived under the rope, uplifted the casket and returned.

'It *is* the casket! Hide it under your cloak, Bina. Walk slowly back the way we came, as though nothing has happened. Don't run, whatever you do!'

Round the gallery they proceeded once more, meeting the unsuspecting attendant. Down the stairway into the hall, through the main door, and into the street. As they crossed the road, Bina uttered a little moan. Suddenly she began to run, and they had to run with her. Down Chambers Street to the Bridges, then, at a traffic block, she swung onto a down-town bus. The boys scrambled on behind her as the bus moved off.

'I told you not to run,' panted Simon.

'Whatever possessed you?' Malcolm asked.

'He — he saw us.' Bina's voice was unlike itself. 'He's after us.'

'What did I tell you?' Simon said. 'Where did you see him?'

'Downstairs, just after the seismograph.' She licked dry lips. 'I wanted to be sure, so I hung back. You've gone on about it so much — I thought I was imagining things.'

'But you're certain it was him.'

Again she nodded, shuddering. 'He was behind a pillar, watching us. He had one of those big-rimmed black hats on, so I couldn't see his eyes properly, but I know he was looking at me.' She covered her face with her hands.

'Did he follow us up to the gallery?'

'I don't know — I think so. I felt him watching, though I didn't see him. I'm certain he saw us take it.' She began to sob. 'I'm frightened. I — I think I'm going mad.'

'Stop it, Bina. Stop that at once!' Simon took both her hands. 'People are looking.'

'He's got through to her in some way, when she wasn't under our protection,' Malcolm said slowly. He looked out of the window. 'Come on, we have to change here. We'd better keep her between us — she might run off.' They squeezed to the door. Bina was weeping openly now, and an old woman with a shopping bag called out: 'Shame on youse boys!'

In Princes Street she eluded them again, making for the Gardens. They ran down the steps by the Floral Clock after her. It was getting dark. Above them, the Castle floated blue, there was a low mist rising. They caught her, dragged her back to the bus stop.

'Give me the casket. I'll put it under my coat, and then you won't feel he's after you.'

'Take it then! Take it!'

She thrust it at them and was off like a cat in the dark. One moment she was beside them, the next she had gone, disappearing into the crowds of homeward-going sales shoppers.

They pounded after her in the direction of the West End. After a hundred yards they stopped.

'She might be anywhere — do you realise that? She might have crossed the street, or gone down into the Gardens — anything!'

'Bet you she's gone home.'

'What about trying the key?'

'No use. It's stone cold.'

Simon frowned. 'If only she hadn't panicked. That's what worries me. She was — almost crazy. If he has her in his power, he could make her do almost anything.'

A car drew up beside them. It was a vintage Rolls Royce with a uniformed chauffeur at the wheel. The lights were dimly burning. Mrs Clarke leaned forward and wound down the window.

'Get in, boys,' she ordered.

They opened the door. As they sat down beside her, Simon handed over the casket, and she slipped it under the fur rug.

The car drew away.

CHAPTER THIRTEEN

They drove slowly, silently. Mrs Clarke's face beneath the fur
hat was pale. She put the casket in her muff. Eventually they
reached an elegant house in Heriot Row, and the car drew to a
standstill. The chauffeur opened the door for them, then ran up
the steps and pulled a bell at the front door.

In a minute a maid in a long black dress with a white apron and
a frilly cap with streamers opened the door. She took the boys'
coats and Mrs Clarke's cloak. Then she showed them into a long,
firelit drawing-room.

Mrs Clarke motioned the boys to sit down. She removed the
casket from her muff and set it upon the small table, where the
boys were able to see it properly for the first time. It gleamed in the
firelight, and they could see its interwoven design of flowers and
symbolic birds. After what seemed a long time, Mrs Clarke sank
into a low chair by the fire.

'Now, at last, it is safe to speak,' she said. 'I have brought you
back here to 1917 because in this way I hope we may be
undisturbed for a little while. Yet it is only in this house that we
have time travelled.'

'The car . . .' began Simon.

'So many people these days have vintage cars that it causes little
comment. Now, we must discuss our next move, for time is getting
short.'

'What about the Captain?'

'The Captain, my dear Malcolm, is occupied elsewhere for the

106

moment. He was misled for a little into thinking Bina had the casket.'

'So she is in danger . . .'

'She is not without protection, however; none of us are. It is very difficult to reach her at the moment — she is not putting out any mental call for help, and until she does that it is not easy to find her.'

'It's all our fault,' burst out Malcolm. 'We ought to be out looking for her right now! She may be in terrible danger — we know she's frightened.'

'Yes, that was part of the problem.' With a sigh, Mrs Clarke removed her fur hat and laid it on a table beside her. 'Bina panicked — and that left her mind defenceless and vulnerable. It was easy for the Captain to take control of her.'

'Isn't there anything we can do?'

'Cerainly there is something we can do. I have contacted the Knights, and with their help we are encircling her in a ring of light — the most powerful protection there is. You can help, too. Send the light out now! Say her name three times.'

Mrs Clarke rose and held out the strange star she wore around her neck. They all fixed their gaze upon it, and repeated Bina's name. As they did so, it seemed to glow, reach a peak of intensity, and die down. A clock struck six with spangled notes.

'You know, Malcolm, you are not concentrating,' Mrs Clarke said sharply.

'I'm sorry, but it does seem that there's a more practical way —'

'Perhaps you want to be out searching for her? Listen, my child, Bina is not awake to anything at present. We have been able to save her from death, but what exactly has happened to her is not yet clear.'

'What's the use of trying any more then?' Malcolm snorted. 'And all for that — that beastly little box!'

'You, neither of you realise the importance of that beastly little box, as you call it,' Mrs Clarke reproved him. 'Come, you are late. Your uncle will be worrying about you, and I believe that news of

Bina awaits you at home. Remember that the Knights and I are with you. You must hold her in the circle of light all the time. The next few days are vital. And you must promise me something. Promise that, no matter what happens, you will not act impulsively on your own, or you yourselves will be in great danger, and we will have failed yet again. Promise!'

They promised and she led them out again to the hall, taking their coats from a chair.

'How are we to know what to do and when?' Simon asked.

'Keep hold of the key. If it remains cold and dead, that is a sign to do nothing. If it grows warm, act on your intuition. I will try to contact you again. Now, close your eyes and take my hands. Think of number twelve Linlithgow Avenue. Think of the year, the day, and the hour you should be in. . . Think. . .'

The humming began and the whole scene faded out before their eyes. When it reformed they were on their own doorstep. The light shone through the panels beside the door, and when they rang, their uncle burst out, in a great state of agitation, bouncing up and down like a ball.

'Where on earth have you two been? I was about to call the police! How did you come to let Bina go off on her own? Answer me!'

'She ran off — we couldn't stop her. What's happened, has she been found?'

'Is she at home? Can we see her?'

'*Home?*' squeaked Uncle Henry. '*Home?* She's had a terrible accident and has been taken to the hospital!'

'Thank heavens we know where she is!'

'Are you out of your mind boy? She was run over — do you understand? Run over by a bus. She is unconscious, her parents are with her now.'

'Unconscious? Oh God, how awful!'

'How did it happen — where?'

'The police say at the corner of Lothian Road and Fountain-bridge.'

'She must have been running home the quickest way she knew.'

'How is she injured?'

'In the head — serious head injuries,' Uncle Henry told them.

'She was terrified, you see she was running away from *him*. From the Captain. He thought she had the casket — well, she did at first —'

'We tried to hold her, but she just sprinted away —'

Their uncle sat down. 'You had better tell me the whole story.'

* * *

In a small side ward off a bigger ward in the Infirmary, Bina lay in a small white bed with a shaded light over her. Her head was cocooned in bandages. A nurse stood beside her taking her pulse, and her father watched from the foot of the bed, while her mother sat, head bowed, sniffing into a large paper handkerchief. A doctor and sister entered; the father asked a question.

'It's impossible to tell yet, Mr Henderson,' was the reply.

Bina's mother began to cry. Her husband put an arm round her. Bina, on the bed, remained utterly still beneath her bandages; she did not seem even to breathe.

* * *

Later that same evening, Mrs Frazer appeared at twelve Linlithgow Avenue, accompanied by her dog and a small suitcase. The whole story was repeated to her after supper.

'So that's your tale, is it?' she remarked.

'Don't you believe us?'

'Oh, I believe you all right. But of all the crazy stupidity. Going off like that on a fool's errand without telling your uncle or anyone where you were going, and taking the poor girl with you! Of course *I* know why she went.'

'She didn't want to be left out. She was keen to come in the end.'

'Keen to come! I'm sure she was!' Their grandmother looked with contempt at her young relations. 'She isn't interested in the search for that casket — and she mistrusts Mistress Clarke as much as I do, I'm sure! No, it's young Simon who's put a spell on her.'

'What are you talking about, Gran?'

'You know very well what I mean, Simon. You were flattered by her attention, and you encouraged her. You wanted to show off your cleverness — you were aware of the risk and you took it! Well, look what's come of it.'

'It wasn't like that, honestly.'

'We couldn't have stopped her coming — she's terrifically strong-willed —' Malcolm defended his cousin.

Ada came in to clear away the supper dishes. 'Dinna tell *me*,' she muttered, clashing plates.

'Don't tell you *what*, woman?' shouted Uncle Henry irritably. 'If you've something to say, say it — don't mumble!'

Ada raised her head. 'Dinna tell me youse lads did naething tae scare the lassie! She's nae easy feart.'

'I swear we didn't, Ada. She saw — she thought she saw something that frightened her and she ran off before we could stop her.'

'That's no like Bina. She aye had a guid head on her shoulders.' Ada fixed them with a boot-button glance. 'It's a' they buiks she's been reading since you boys came. Terrible stuff. A' aboot warlocks and witches and ghosties! Minnie Beaton, she cleans for Mrs Henderson, she tellt me that the lassie's been waking and crying out in her sleep! And you, Mr Gilchrist — sitting in the dark and holding see-ances. It's nae right. I'll need tae tell Mrs Henderson.'

'That's quite enough, Ada.'

'And the polis were asking questions, so I hear. They wanted to find out what made her run like that right into the face of the bus. The driver hadna a chance to pull up. A woman on the corner of Bread Street saw it all. She says the lassie rin as though the deevil were ahint her, and nivver looked right or left.'

'Ada!'

'Very weel, Mr Gilchrist. But it's a queer business altogether — folks in this house seem to hae taken leave of their senses. Bells ringing wi'oot wire and —' she took a handkerchief out of her apron and blew her nose loudly.

'That will do, Ada!' Mrs Frazer spoke quietly but with authority. 'We know you are upset.'

'I was right fond of the lassie, she was aye in and oot the place, and now it's visiting any time at the hospital, so Minnie tells me. A bad sign.'

Mrs Frazer approached her with firm steps and took her arm.

'Now listen, Ada, I have kept quiet up to now because this isn't my house. But you have spoken out of turn, and of matters that don't concern you. What do you think old Mrs Gilchrist would say if she could see you now?'

The sobbing died down. 'Yes'm.'

'You spoke very rudely to Mr Gilchrist just now.'

'Sorry, sir. Sorry m'm.'

'I know you're upset and frightened, but that's no excuse! Now the best thing you can do is go away quietly and say a prayer for poor little Bina, and stop thinking the worst. And don't forget the pepper pot.'

Simon opened the door for Ada and the tray and closed it softly.

Mrs Frazer took her cigarettes out of her handbag and lit one. 'There's going to be trouble, Harry. Mrs Clarke always brings trouble. And what about the casket the boys stole? I expect there will be an enquiry as to how that got taken right under the eyes of a museum attendant. He probably saw the children hanging about and got a description of them. I suppose that hasn't occurred to you?'

'It has, Lucy, but I have a shrewd idea that it was never part of the Museum collection. I think this was just a temporary hiding place. Of course I would not dream of asking, but I suspect if one did, one would find nobody knew a thing about it, it would not be listed or anything. After all, they were rearranging that room and nothing was in a fixed place.'

Mrs Frazer inhaled smoke, to Malcolm's disgust, and blew out tiny rings. 'I'm not so sure. Why was it left out in the open like that, if it was so precious?'

'Maybe it had been in a locked cupboard somewhere else in the Museum, and the curator who was setting out this room just happened to remember it and thought it would look right. Who knows?'

'Nothing happens by chance,' Simon put in. 'He was probably influenced by someone or something to put it there.'

'So it wasn't as safe as the Captain supposed? Yet he must have had an inkling that it was in danger, otherwise why did he choose that moment to appear?'

'That Mistress Clarke,' their grandmother's voice cut like a pair of scissors across the boys' reasoning, 'She had no business involving Malcolm and Simon and that poor little girl! Harry, stop looking like a bird with the moult. What you need is a good dram.'

Against his protests she rose, went to the whisky decanter on the sideboard and poured a generous dose into a small tumbler. 'Here, take this!'

The boys sat in gloomy silence.

'It won't help Bina or anyone else for you two to sit there like graven images. If you imagine that your fairy godmother is going to tap at the window and come in all starry-eyed and covered with snowflakes to wave her wand and rescue us from the mess we're in, you're quite mistaken. This is one time we will have to act on our own.'

'We're not on our own, Gran. We've got the key, and Mrs Clarke and the Knights are helping us.' Malcolm looked steadily at his grandmother. She stubbed out her cigarette.

'We were told to hold her in the light,' he said.

'And what does *that* mean?'

'To see a sort of protective circle of light all round her — by telepathy you know.'

'You'd be better off saying your prayers,' Mrs Frazer said.

'I should say it was much the same thing,' Uncle Henry told her quietly. His sister looked at him, but found nothing to say. She asked the boys if they would take the dog for a walk; then changed her mind and said she would do it herself. 'What a pity your uncle has no television,' she said. 'It would be quite a distraction.'

* * *

It was late at night; Malcolm slept soundly, but Simon tossed and turned in his sleep. He was dreaming. Floating in the night sky above old Edinburgh, looking down on the ramparts of the Castle, on the Crown tower of St Giles, on the Assembly Rooms, the Mound, all floating like himself in moonlight. Suddenly he realised that Malcolm was floating with him, casually. They drifted unhurriedly over the roofs of Waverley Station.

'She said there was very little time left, only three days,' Malcolm remarked, swimming through an eddy of cumulus clouds and emerging over the Canongate.

Simon was annoyed. 'Three days! I never heard her mention three days. What for, in heavens name?'

'Well, Bina's lost, isn't she?' Malcolm floated on his back, puffing gently.

'Lost? No she's not! She's in hospital!'

'She's lost, though,' Malcolm repeated, and seemed to be drifting away from Simon, down towards Holyrood Palace and out of sight. 'Quite, quite lost.'

'She's not lost!' shouted Simon. 'Come back! I tell you she's in hospital!'

And immediately, as he came back to consciousness, he heard Mrs Clarke's voice, somewhere near the ceiling. 'Yes, alas, Simon, she is lost. Her body is in the hospital, but the real part of her is not there. And time is running out. You have only three days in which to find her. Three days.'

'Mrs Clarke! Mrs Clarke!'

Simon leaned out of bed and switched on the lamp. The room was empty, except for Malcolm, who turned over and opened his eyes at the light.

'What's up? Are you ill or something?'

'I had a nightmare.' Simon reached for his glasses. 'A ghastly nightmare,' he repeated. 'Mal, Bina *is* in hospital, isn't she?'

'Of course she is, you know that.'

'It can't have been a dream, though! I heard Mrs Clarke's voice. Just now, from somewhere up there near the ceiling.'

'Saying what?'

'Three days. That's what she said. We've only got three days left. Did *you* hear her mention three days?'

'No, I didn't. Three days for what?'

'To find the real part of Bina, and bring her back — into her body that's unconscious at the hospital. The Captain's hidden her — the real Bina, I mean.'

'What are you talking about?' Malcolm demanded.

'I'm just telling you what Mrs Clarke said.'

'Well, I'm going to sleep.' Malcolm leaned over and switched off the light. 'Goodnight. Pleasant dreams. I hope you don't have any more nightmares.'

Simon leapt out of bed and shook him. 'Wake up you lazy slob! Don't you realise that Bina's life is in danger.' He turned the light on again. 'We have to save her. Where's the key?'

'Where it usually is, round my neck.'

'OK, we'll use it to concentrate on, like Mrs Clarke told us. Try to see Bina, in the hospital, surrounded by light. And then imagine that light, like a laser beam, going out to find her, the real her, and bring her back.'

With a sigh, Malcolm sat up in bed, holding the key, and closed his eyes in an effort to concentrate. In a few minutes his head lolled forward and he yawned deeply. 'It's no use, Si, I just can't see any sort of light. I'm so slee- sleepy.' He rolled over, pulling up the bedclothes.

Simon leapt out of bed and ran over to the fitted basin. He took a sponge and filled it with cold water, which he applied with a smart slap to Malcolm's face. With a shout, Malcolm rose dripping from the bed and hurled himself on the smaller boy. Suddenly, they were both wide awake.

While Malcolm towelled himself dry, Simon, wrapped in his duvet, for it was bitterly cold and the central heating was off, explained his theory.

'I think it's something like electricity. You can't send the current out direct on the grid from the huge power stations into our houses without stepping the voltage down and earthing it, using sub-stations and pylons and so on, right down to a five-amp plug. And that's what we are — the small plugs. But without us the big powerhouses — the Knights, whoever they are — can't reach people, not successfully. That's why it's absolutely essential for us to do our bit.'

Malcolm was interested. 'How did you work that one out?'

'Oh it just came to me,' said Simon airily. 'Never mind that now. Fix your mind on the key and concentrate. Close your eyes and think about Bina in the Light.'

* * *

A point of light came in a land of darkness. Bina watched it without interest. How peaceful to sit in the dark, making no effort. The light grew. It began to irritate her, like the prick of a pin. She tried to turn her head away so that she couldn't see it any more. After an aeon, instead of going away the light increased in size, making a hole in the dark, the size of a saucer. She made dim efforts to shut it out.

'Where — am I?' murmured the Bina-in-a-dream person.

There came no answer, nor was she anxious to hear one. It pleased her to continue asking her questions aloud. 'What am I? I feel no heat, no cold. I have no body, no shape. There is no distance, no time, nothing . . .'

Idly she looked through the hole the light had made. She thought that down a long corridor shapes moved and voices called. They were too dim, too far off to trouble her. The light dimmed to a point but remained. She drifted, floating on a dark sea.

* * *

Malcolm was dreaming now. He found himself in a luxurious bedroom belonging, apparently, to Mrs Clarke. Anyway, there she was, seated before her dressing-table, in a long robe of red velvet, brushing her red-gold hair. The fire danced on her white arms, brushing, lifting and falling, and threw dancing shadows of arms up to the ceiling. Malcolm curled himself up on a thick white rug, hypnotised by the brushing, the crackling fire, the warmth and the scent of violets which filled the room.

'Now, Malcolm, this will not do! You have fallen asleep again!' Mrs Clarke set down her brush and began to plait, strand after strand reaching her waist.

'Oh, let me stay here! It's so warm and safe.'

'Only the gods can afford to waste time,' she told him severely, tying the plait with an apricot ribbon. 'It has no existence for them, but it is not on the side of mortals and never has been.'

'We did concentrate on Bina, honestly. But one can't do it all the time. It's so difficult, and one's mind keeps wandering. I keep thinking — what's the use?'

Time now appeared to Malcolm, in the corner of the room, like a disagreeable grandfather clock, with a painted face which showed the moon and the sun — very similar to the one in the upstairs hall at Linlithgow Avenue. The tick now sounded remorselessly, relentlessly, drowning all other sound in the room. Suddenly it cleared its throat and struck three with deep, muffled, doomful strokes.

'You must be faithful, Malcolm! Anything worthwhile is difficult! Bring your mind back. Fill it with light. Just think of yourself as a channel for all the power we are pouring through you to Bina. We can't do without you. You must see that. Now you must go back, Malcolm. Go back to bed and help Simon!'

'One day has almost gone, though, hasn't it? And — Mrs Clarke?'

'Yes?'

'The Captain — he's holding Bina as a sort of hostage, isn't he, to make you give back the casket so that they can seize the substance when it is unsealed?'

'I fear so, Malcolm, I very much fear so. And I can read your thought. It is that I should return the casket to him in order to free Bina. And in that case our long struggle must begin all over again, and perhaps not be resolved before great tragedy comes upon the world and all its people.'

'I don't believe you'd let her die!' cried Malcolm.

Mrs Clarke stood up, seeming to grow so tall she touched the ceiling. The whole room dissolved in scarves of mist around her. 'Alas, Malcolm,' her voice came from a distance, 'it is out of my hands. The substance is only sealed for another forty hours. After that, it and the world, are vulnerable.'

'But do you mean that . . .'

The dream faded suddenly, as though cut off with sharp scissors. No longer could he see the mirror, the fire or the dressing-table beside which Mrs Clarke had been standing. Instead, he was at sea. On a ship, a great sailing ship, and he was in the rigging. The top and main sails were spread, the flag it flew was the skull and crossbones. All the cannon on the upper and lower deck began to fire. Boom! Boom! Boom! Boom! Just like a clock striking.

All the guns were firing at — yes — he could see it now — firing at a small, graceful schooner. It was hit — it turned on its side, sinking low in the water, and on it Malcolm could just decipher the words: *The Robina Henderson, Leith*. Immediately, he projected a ray of light towards the schooner. He saw the ray going out from his own heart. It made a ring round the little ship, protecting it. Now he had left the rigging and was floating in the air above the schooner, maintaining the ring of light about it. The firing stopped. The great ship withdrew; and as it did so he could read the name emblazoned on her side: *The Nostradamus*. The dream faded. Malcolm woke, in January daylight, remembering.

CHAPTER FOURTEEN

It was breakfast time, and the only individual who seemed to be enjoying himself was Joss the terrier. He was wolfing down the bacon that no one else had the appetite to eat.

There was silence, except for the scraping of toast. Uncle Henry returned from the telephone with trotting steps and a grim moustache.

'Bina is still unconscious. She is no better, but no worse.'

'Ask Ada for some more hot water, please, Malcolm,' said Mrs Frazer. Malcolm rose and picked up the jug. He turned at the door. 'How long can a person live if they're unconscious?'

'Months, perhaps years,' their great-uncle replied. 'Marmalade, Simon?'

'No thanks. I knew a boy once when we were in Geneva. He lived for two years after a car crash, but he was a vegetable and had to be fed intravenously.'

'What's that?'

'With tubes.'

'There's no need for such details! Hot water, please, Malcolm!'

Malcolm sped to the kitchen.

'Bina won't be like that, because she won't live so long,' Simon told them. 'Ada says the ward sister told Bina's mother that if there was no improvement in the next two days . . .'

Malcolm returned, overhearing this speech. 'That makes the three days,' he said, setting the jug in front of his grandmother. 'That's what Mrs Clarke said was left to us, before . . .'

118

Mrs Frazer set the teapot down with a jolt. 'Mrs Clarke! She's to blame for everything! Don't speak to me of Mrs Clarke!'

'Lucy,' Uncle Henry said mildly, 'this situation is far too serious for the raking up of old jealousies.'

'Jealousies? I've never been jealous of *her* — I just can't thole her, that's all.' She poured hot water into the pot and replaced the lid. Then she turned to her grandsons. 'And how did you get hold of this nonsense about three days — I suppose Mrs Clarke told you in a dream last night! No, don't answer, I can see by your faces that she did! As for this ward sister — there's something very peculiar about *that* tale. A hospital sister is a very responsible person. She would never have told Mary Henderson there was no hope for Bina after three days. No, this is another invention of Ada's and that gossiping Mrs Beaton next door.'

'What's important is that the girl's life is in serious danger,' Uncle Henry said. 'If we can help in any way we must do so. Let's leave Mrs Clarke out of it.'

'But we can't leave her out of it!' Simon threw down his napkin. 'She's the one who's masterminding the rescue operation — trying to save Bina's life. We have to take her word for it to work! She told us what to do; we have to keep holding Bina in our thoughts, imagining her protected by a ray of white light, until . . .' his voice trailed away.

'Until what?' Mrs Frazer asked. 'It all sounds like a load of claptrap to me!'

'Look,' Simon said, desperately. He pushed his spectacles up into his shock of dark hair. 'I know this sounds weird to you — it does to me too, but I just somehow *know* it's right. The Captain — don't interrupt, just *listen* to me for a minute — the Captain has somehow established a hold over the *real* part of Bina — her soul, no that's not right, call it her individuality. . . . Not her spirit, that's indestructible. Anyway, the Bina that's lying in the Infirmary is a sort of shell, and we've got to find the other part and link the two together again. Before it's too late,' he added.

His grandmother rose and started to pile the dishes together.

'Simon, I think you have been under a lot of strain recently. We all have. I think you and Malcolm should go for a nice walk this morning, and perhaps we could all go to the cinema this afternoon. I think there's a very good picture on at the Odeon.' She clashed knives together, scraping the congealed remains of bacon. Uncle Henry rose, for once he seemed to tower over his sister.

'Lucy, be quiet! You were always the bossy one. You always knew best. This time I must insist that you listen to me. In a way it was your fault that this whole thing happened — yes, yes, I know, just hear me out. We opened that — that Pandora's box and let out all the devils. I was weak, I should not have let you persuade me. We brought the Captain into our street, and we endangered, not just our own lives, but God knows how many others. Don't you think it's time we tried to do something to make up for all that?'

Mrs Frazer was still fighting. 'I don't know how you can credit all this nonsense!' she cried. 'But if you do, then surely there's a simple answer. Get your Mrs Clarke to give the Captain back his casket. Then Bina will be safe, and we'll be finished with the whole business.'

Malcolm, his face red, leaned forward. 'Don't you see, Gran, if we did that, then in two days the substance will be released and there will be no casket to contain it in. In the wrong hands its effects would be stronger than a thousand atomic bombs. The whole world might be destroyed!'

Slowly his grandmother sat down. Her lips were pinched together. She looked from one to another of her relations and found no support anywhere.

'What do you want me to do?' she asked, sounding defeated.

Simon sat down again too, pushing his chair back from the table. Malcolm occupied himself on the hearthrug with Joss, keeping the dog — who had been disturbed by the raised voices — as quiet as possible.

'We just want you to help us. Uncle Henry too. We have to

project this light, like I told you, around her. We do it mentally, it's a sort of telepathy. The light acts as a kind of protective wall, so the Captain can't get at her. Malcolm and I did it last night — it's pretty hard to keep concentrating so we used the key as a kind of symbol. And while we do it, we have to keep saying her name.'

'No, we don't *keep* saying it, Si, we have to say it three times, that's all,' Malcolm interjected from the hearthrug. 'While we're concentrating.'

'And how often are we supposed to do this?'

'I'm not really certain. Obviously we can't do it all the time — we'd be totally exhausted. How about every three or four hours?'

'Day and night?'

'I don't know — I think at night our subconscious takes over, as long as we think strongly enough about it before we go to sleep.'

'What kind of light?' Uncle Henry wanted to know.

'A very strong white light — like a laser beam or a spotlight. A — what's the word — an *incandescent* light.'

'We can begin now, it's just on nine o'clock. After that at twelve, then at three, at six, and so on.' The old man sounded quite excited. His thin white hair was standing up untidily; absent-mindedly he smoothed it down.

'I suggest we get the table cleared, then we can use this room. I'll ask Ada not to disturb us. She can have Joss in the kitchen, God knows she spoils him enough.' Ever practical, Mrs Frazer lifted the piled plates. At the door she turned. 'I'm still not certain what you're trying to achieve, but since you all feel so strongly about it, I'll do my best to help you.' She went out.

'What do you think we should do, Uncle Henry?' Malcolm asked. 'Sit round holding hands, like a seance?'

'No — I don't approve of seances. They can raise elements that are best left undisturbed. I think we should just sit quietly, and concentrate as hard as we can.' Simon and his grandmother returned and closed the door behind them.

'Let's begin then, shall we?' Malcolm suggested when the grandmother returned.

The square clock on the mantelpiece struck nine.

They began by saying Bina's name.

* * *

Bina spoke her thoughts into the darkness. 'Leave me alone, can't you? Alone . . . alone . . . alone.'

The darkness was not so black.

She saw that she was in a little boat, drifting upon a calm, grey sea. Neither night nor day nor any living thing moved about her. She was content to let the tide take her where it would.

Then she felt a pain, sharp as a knitting needle.

Strong light poured down upon her, piercing through some point in her breast that was truly herself. She wriggled, trying to escape, wishing herself so small that the light could not find her. But the light was now accompanied by a sound, shrill as a whistle. Sound and light became at once almost unbearable pain. She cried out.

No sound came.

Her dry lips, her aching throat, made no voice. Her one wish was to escape, to hide from the light, the sound, the pain they made.

So she left the boat, she sank, sank beneath the cool, dark water. But the light found her, even there. Again she was floating, floating in her little boat. And in the relief from pain, something in Bina gave a faint response, an answering signal to the watchers, no more than a trapped insect. It was a gnat's moan. Light round the boat grew; the drifting stopped, as though an anchor were cast down, tethering her craft.

* * *

It was the morning of the next day. The boys and their uncle sat together in his study. Uncle Henry read *The Scotsman*, the boys played Scrabble. Their grandmother had departed with her terrier and her overnight bag three hours ago, promising resignedly to co-operate every three hours. It was raining.

'There!' Simon arranged his letters on the board.

Malcolm peered. 'There's no such word as "durum".'

'Yes there is. It's a kind of wheat — it's made into flour which is used for making spaghetti.I've seen it growing in the States . . .'

'All right, all right. We know you've been all over the world. Anyway, I'm going to look it up in the dictionary. If it's not in there you can't have it.' The clock struck twelve. They rose and stood in silence.

Malcolm took out the key and held it up. The ritual was repeated, beginning with the name said three times. There was a pause. Their uncle cleared his throat.

'I wonder if the same thought has occurred to you as it has to me?' he asked.

'That what we're doing may not be enough?' enquired Simon.

'Exactly so. Mmm. Yes.'

'I feel that too,' Malcolm put in. 'Time's getting so short.'

'Perhaps Mrs Clarke's prompted this feeling on your part, although for some reason she's not allowed to help us in person,' murmured Uncle Henry.

'What do you think we should do then?'

'Clear that game of yours off the table. Now, Malcolm, take the key and put it in the centre. Pull the curtains. Simon, turn off all the lights except for that little reading lamp. Now, let's sit down quietly round the table.'

'I thought you didn't approve of seances?'

'Desperate situations require desperate measures,' came the reply. 'Anyway, this isn't a seance, none of us is a medium as far as I am aware. Now, close your eyes, and concentrate on asking, very strongly, for help and guidance.'

They waited a minute. Nothing.

'Perhaps some music would help. Malcolm, what have you got on that cassette player of yours? Pop music I expect.'

'No, as a matter of fact, Mozart.'

'Put it on.'

'I'll have to go and get it — it's in the bedroom.'

Malcolm left the room and returned with a minature cassette deck, complete with speakers, his mother's Christmas present.

Kneeling, he touched a button and, after a pause, music flooded the room. They concentrated on the key. Very faintly, it began to glow. The room faded away and the two boys found themselves once again in the strange vaulted chamber. Facing them, and alone this time, was the Knight-King. He did not smile.

'My children, you have something to ask?'

Simon's mouth was dry. He tried to speak.

'Do not be afraid, my son.'

He found his voice. 'Sir, we feel, all of us . . . that there is something else we ought to be doing. Something more. But we don't know what it is. Will you help us?'

'You are doing well. You have forged the first — the most important link. Do not worry, you will soon be shown what comes next. Remember that your strength is not your own. As long as you hold fast to the key, all will be well.'

'But time is getting so short —'

'When the test comes, you will not fail. Dwell in the consciousness of the Force Field of the Star of Light!'

The scene faded and they became aware of music. They came back into the study again.

'Malcolm — Simon — are you all right?' Their uncle was looking anxiously at them.

'We're OK. What happened?'

'You tell *me* happened. I wasn't with you.' Uncle Henry tried to sound cheerful, but was obviously disappointed. 'You seemed to go into a trance of some kind.'

'Yes, we saw the King — the Knight-King,' Malcolm said dreamily.

'I was scared,' Simon said. 'No, that's not the right word.'

'Awed?'

'Yes, I suppose so.'

'And did you ask what we should do?'

'Yes, he told us that we were doing well, that we would be shown what to do next.'

'He told us that there was going to be some kind of test,' Malcolm said, getting up to turn off the Mozart. 'But he didn't say when.'

'I'd better ring your grandmother and get her to come back here.' Uncle Henry shuffled to the door. 'How much I'd have liked to — but it's not to be. No second chance. Anyway, I'm too old now, useless.'

'You're not useless, Uncle Henry — far from it. We have to have someone here to protect us,' Malcolm said kindly.

'It's odd, you know,' Simon volunteered to his cousin. 'Just before we came back here, I felt I knew exactly where Bina's real self was. And now it's all vanished. I can't recall a thing!'

'I'm hungry,' Malcolm said. 'I haven't felt hungry for two days, but now I could eat a rhinoceros. Let's get Ada to make us some scrambled eggs.'

CHAPTER FIFTEEN

Bina was beneath the waves, washed gently by the tide. How pleasant to ebb first this way, then that. Great fish swam past her. How brilliant their colours were — scarlet, purple and gold — or, argent, cramoisie, vert..

'I would like to stay here always,' dreamed Bina.

She floated above great rocks, beautiful, of many colours and forms. Tiny creatures clung to the ledges and crevices, sea-anemones, silver limpets, vermillion starfish. Like firework stars, shoals of brilliant fish burst on her vision, all live, all sounding notes of music, making chords, scales of infinite harmony.

'That cruel ray of light can't reach me here,' decided Bina, 'I am hidden completely. Even the crabs, scuttling sideways, the eels, the immense shadowy sharks above can't harm me. I have no shape, no sound, no name. I am what I will myself to be . . . Nothing! . . . Someone is calling a name, but I have no name. I am perfectly happy. So happy . . .' She watched a school of most exquisite, transparent jellyfish floating like fronded domes above her, changing their shape with every movement, from pancake to bell.

'Oh, they're lit up inside!' she exclaimed with delight and surprise. 'They glow like roses — their fringes make a tinkling sound as they comb the water! How beautiful! How wonderful! I shall stay here for ever!'

Without willing it, she found she had risen with the jellyfish and seemed to follow them. Now, on either side, she was accompanied by soals of fish, rounded, deep indigo and orange-striped, with

126

little mouths opening and shutting in question. Bubbles rose from them, plink, plink, like harp strings plucked. Because she was not willing to make the smallest effort, she allowed them to crowd close, to press against and sometimes even to pass through her, as though her body had no existence. 'Oh well, let them go!' she laughed.

So she played at rising and falling with the currents, just as the fish did; and found it most pleasant. Yet now a larger fish, with big protuberant eyes and open mouth filled with razor teeth, loomed beside her, bringing with it a crew of strange beings, half-transparent mermen, with fish tails and heads of worm-like hair, wriggling with a life of its own. These creatures stared at Bina with cold, impertinent eyes, then closed in upon her, pinching, scratching and mocking soundlessly with green, sidelong glances.

Fear began in Bina. 'Go away!' But her voice was lost. 'Get lost!' she squeaked. 'Ow, that hurt! Stop pinching — what nails you have — like claws!'

They paid no attention, but only came closer, touching her in a cold and slimy fashion. Now the monster fish approached, its great mouth widening.

'This won't do at all — I shall cease to exist if this goes on much longer!' gasped Bina, trying to retreat. She began to make a very feeble effort to raise what was left of herself out of their clutches. Yet the more she struggled, and very weak struggles they were, the more like octopuses became the mermen, the more their tentacle-like arms and even their wormy hair seemed to wind themselves round her frail being, ready to crush the last drop of life out of her and hand her over to the waiting monster to devour.

In a flash she realised that unless help came immediately, this was the end of her. So, with the last of her weakened willpower she collected herself to send out from the inmost pinhead of her person a cry for help as thin as a mosquito's whine. And, almost immediately, her cry was answered.

It came in the form of a ray of light; intense, blinding, penetrating the darkness of the water right down to where she lay pinioned, dissolving all her attackers, and raising her up, up towards the surface.

Bina opened her eyes. She was in darkness, but a brisk voice close beside her remarked, 'Now then, dear — you are all right.'

And then came her mother's voice, and she felt her mother's hand on hers. 'Bina! It's mummy! Oh my darling girl!' She felt a face, wet with tears, kissing her, but she could see nothing.

'Mummy! Oh mummy!'

'It's all right, lamb, Daddy and I are here.'

'Daddy?'

'Here I am pet. Don't fret yourself. You had a wee accident and you're in hospital, but you're going to be all right now.'

Bina burst into tears; they rolled down between the bandages. 'It's *not* all right — I'm *not* in hospital — I don't know where I am! *I can't see you!*'

A man's voice, a doctor perhaps, spoke. 'She's a little confused. I think that's enough for now. We have to make an examination. Come back in an hour or so.'

'But this not seeing, doctor? Is it — I mean . . .'

'Oh, we won't worry unduly, it's too early to say.'

'Don't go, mummy, don't go,' wailed Bina. 'Please don't let her go!' There was a whispering and shuffling. Someone said, 'Don't talk then, Mrs Henderson,' and she felt her mother's hand once more holding hers.

* * *

They were all waiting in the study, the boys staring listlessly out of the window. Uncle Henry put the telephone down.

'Well, it seems she's recovered consciousness. She's been asking for you two. You're to go to the hospital to see her, but mind you don't say anything that might get her excited or upset. She's still in a critical state, and there appears to be some problem with her eyes.'

'What problem?'

'She can't see anything — it's probably only a temporary blindness caused by shock. That quite often happens after a head injury. Now you'd better go and get ready. Mr Henderson's calling here in about twenty minutes to take you to the Infirmary.'

'I am sure it's nothing to worry about,' their grandmother said consolingly. She had returned, in answer to a telephone call from her brother, complaining that she felt like a yo-yo with all this to-ing and fro-ing. 'After all, the main thing is that she's recovered consciousness. And you were the first people she asked to see. She'll get her sight back in a few days, I'm sure.'

'It's not the child's sight that's at fault, Lucy,' came Mrs Clarke's voice from somewhere near the ceiling.

'Lalla!' shouted Uncle Henry. 'Where are you? Where have you been? We have needed you desperately.'

'No questions' — Mrs Clarke added 'please' as an after-thought. 'I, too, have been busy. Everything depends upon the next few hours. Malcolm and Simon's job is to find out where Bina's true self is. Obviously she is imprisoned somewhere and you must do your best to get a description from her — however vague — of where she supposes herself to be. Try and get her to tell you what she sees, or hears or feels.'

'Surely you can help us by giving us some hint?'

'If I knew, Harry, then of course I would,' Mrs Clarke's voice was fainter, further off. 'But only you, only you can find her now. Be resolute, keep calm. Keep — on — holding — her — in — the — Light.'

'But, Mrs Clarke —'

There was silence.

'A lot of help that was,' said their grandmother. 'Even Joss is disgusted. Poor beast, he's growling and his hair is standing on end!'

'Go and get your coats on,' ordered Uncle Henry. 'I hear Mr Henderson hooting for you. And, Malcolm — be sure you have the key safe.'

***

They were in Bina's little cubicle in the hospital.

129

The sister left them, warning them, 'Talk quietly! Nothing to excite her, please. Ten minutes only.'

They looked in shocked disbelief at the white face on the pillow in its helmet of bandages. They went up to the bed. Bina made no movement, her eyes were closed.

'Is she asleep?'

'I don't know.' Simon went close. 'Bina, it's us. Simon and Malcolm.' There was no movement. Malcolm pulled the key out of his pocket. He seemed uncertain for a moment, then leant forward and touched her; first on the top of her head, then on the throat, then on the heart.

'Why did you do that?'

'I'm not quite sure,' Malcolm said, 'but I seemed to hear someone telling me to do it. Look!'

Slowly Bina's eyes opened, as though the lashes were stuck together. She swallowed, breathing hard. 'It's still so — dark — in here. Who's that?'

'Simon and Malcolm.'

She breathed fast, then held out a long, thin, hot hand which Simon grasped. 'Oh save me! Save me, please! I'm so frightened!'

'We'll save you, Bina, but you must tell us where you are.' Simon tried to make his voice calm, reassuring.

'I — I don't know, how am I supposed to tell? I can't. I can't —'

Malcolm held up the key. It seemed to glow, faintly.

'What can you see now?'

'I see light, a little light.'

Malcolm handed the key to his cousin, took out a stubby red notebook and a biro. He began to take notes.

'What do you feel, Bina?' Simon demanded.

'Sick. Everything's rocking, rocking up and down, round and round. Stop it! Stop it! Oh, that's better.'

'Come on,' urged Simon. 'Just give us something, anything!'

'I can't seem to move . . . can't see anything very much either. Wait a minute . . . I think I'm in a room — it's very dim, as though

I was looking through glass. That lamb . . . so stupid . . . never really liked it . . .' Her voice died away again.

'Try, Bina, try!'

'People shouting, men, *He* came and looked at me — huge, sneer-ing . . . I'm frightened. Oh, that rocking's started again . . . I hate it . . .'

Her eyes closed, she moaned a little and fell silent.

'It's no use,' Simon said. 'She's gone off again. Quick, someone's coming. Hide the key.'

It was the ward sister to tell them that time was up. She was followed by Mr and Mrs Henderson.

'Is she unconscious again? She said she felt sick, then she just seemed to go — right off —.' Malcolm sounded worried.

The sister examined Bina. 'No, she's just sleeping. She's still very weak, you know.'

'How is she, sister?'

'A little better.'

'Can we come back tomorrow?' This to Mr Henderson.

'Perhaps. We'll see. Now can you find your own way out? If you would like to wait for me in reception I can take you home in about three-quarters of an hour.'

The boys assured him that they could find their own way back, thanked him, and said they would ring tomorrow to check on Bina's progress. Then they walked quickly, running down flights of stairs and along steam-heated corridors, until at last they reached the main entrance and came out into the cold dampness of the street.

They stopped running, coming up the incline and crossing Lauriston Place.

'Did you — write it all down?' gasped Simon.

Malcolm nodded, patting his pocket where he had stowed the notebook.

'Let's go into a café and get a cup of tea — then we can go over it and recap.'

They found a suitable place and pushed open the door to a blare of music. When they had carried their slopping cups to a booth as far from the noise as possible, they got out the notebook and pored over the scribbled words.

'Somewhere where she can't move, but she feels as though she is being rocked. Looking through glass, she said.'

'Shop window? No, she saw into a room, not out into a street. And anyway, that wouldn't be rocking up and down. Sounds like a boat . . . pass the sugar, Mal.'

'A *boat* — that's it! Not an ordinary boat — a ship! I bet that's where he's got her, on the *Nostradamus*!'

'Then he must have taken her back in time — the *Nostradamus* is probably on the bottom of the ocean by now. What else did she say . . . something about him sneering at her—that must be the Captain.'

'Yes, huge, she said. That sounds rather as if . . .'

'As if he's somehow shrunk her down in size — yes, I thought of that.' Simon stirred his tea, frowning. 'There's something else that puzzles me — what was that stuff about a sheep, or was it a lamb?'

'A lamb, yes that's right.' Malcolm flicked a page of his notebook. 'Here it is "That lamb — so stupid — never really liked it." I don't understand that either. As far as I know you wouldn't have a lamb on board ship, certainly not a ship like *that*.' They were silent, sipping their tea. Suddenly Simon looked up, his eyes shining with excitement.

'Mal — listen; suppose she's imprisoned in something like an ornament, or a model? She can't move, she's behind glass, she's obviously been shrunk down — it all fits, doesn't it? What can you think of that's likely . . .'

'There's something at the back of my mind,' Malcolm squeezed his eyes shut in concentration, 'but I just can't get it . . . wait a minute . . . wait a minute — *I know!* It's that china shepherdess, the one we saw in the Museum! You remember — she even had a stupid sort of lamb lying at her feet, gazing up at her. That's it! That's got to be it!'

'She was rabbiting on about how she was going to have it in her castle when she married a millionaire, and you said something like "what are you on about — that you really hated it".'

'Yes, that was just about the time she thought she'd spotted the Captain, I expect she was trying to keep her mind off it. And of course, *he* was watching her, so . . .'

'Come on, is the Museum still open?'

Malcolm consulted his watch. 'Should be. But it won't be there, you know. And someone might recognise us from the time we lifted the casket.'

'Well, I'm going to take the risk. Let's go.'

They rose precipitately from the table and made their way out to the twilit, lamplit streets. It was raining. They crossed again, made their way to Chambers Street. Up the steps into the Museum, across the hall, up the curving stairway into the gallery. They searched up and down, with growing impatience.

'I told you it wouldn't be here.'

'Might have been moved — put away.'

No china shepherdess. No ornament in the least like it. At last, coming towards them like an answer to prayer, not the officious attendant (who would, they feared, have recognised them) but a smiling, vague, elderly man who seemed to be some kind of curator with all the time in the world to spare.

'Ah, you are interested in the little Dresden Shepherdess, you say? Not Dresden, I'm afraid, Stoke, but a charming piece all the same. Alas, you will no longer be able to see it. It was on loan, I believe, and has been returned to its owner. Let me see, yes, there you are.'

He pointed to a case where, in a space they had not previously noticed, a card lay neglected. They read: 'Shepherdess, with Garland. Stoke 1760'.

'This card should have been lifted. Most careless, I shall have to have words about that. Yes, the owner collected it — let me see, about three days ago.'

The boys looked at each other.

'I suppose, sit, you wouldn't know his name, or where he could be contacted?'

'Oh, no, I'm afraid I couldn't do that without consulting the records. Why do you want to know, eh? I think, however, he was a foreign gentleman, a captain something or other, I forget the name. He did say that he was going abroad almost immediately and wished to take it with him.'

'Thanks very much, sir.'

'Not at all, not at all. I am sorry I can be of no more help to you. Had you any special reason for being interested? A school project, perhaps? We have some charming . . .'

'It's all right, sir, thank you, we must rush off now, we're late already.' They sped down the gallery, leaving the curator looking after them in a puzzled manner.

'What now?'

Simon leant his aching head against a cool pillar. 'It's twenty past five. Better get out of here before it closes.' They were silent as they walked to the bus stop. Rain reflected from shop fronts and car headlights. As they reached the stop Malcolm spoke.

'He must have time travelled Bina back to 1798 inside the shepherdess and then put her in some cupboard on board the *Nostradamus*. Heaven knows how we can get to her now, and we've only got seven — no, six and a half hours left to midnight.'

Simon nodded miserably. He felt tired and cold. 'It didn't really matter to him whether Bina had the casket or not. He just fastened on her because she panicked, and that meant he could take her over easily. And of course he realised that he could blackmail us through her.'

The bus drew up beside them and they shuffled on board, moving like little old men. When they reached the top deck and sat down, Malcolm burst out: 'She'll have to give the casket back — Mrs C, I mean. There's no other way round it. I just can't stand seeing Bina like she was this afternoon, suffering, and being able to do nothing! We'll have to contact Mrs C when we get back — and tell her. After all we've done our best! We've done all we can!'

Simon was silent. Somehow, he did not think it was going to be that easy.

CHAPTER SIXTEEN

'Inside a china ornament on board the Nostradamus in the year 1798!' exclaimed Uncle Henry. They were all seated in the drawing-room of number twelve Linlithgow Avenue, having just finished an early supper of beans on toast, it being Ada's night off.

'Well, I suppose if we're to go mad in imagination, it might as well be in a big and extravagant way,' remarked their grandmother tartly, as she took out her knitting.

'We have to contact Mrs Clarke,' Malcolm said wearily. 'Tell her we tried, but it's no good. She'll have to give up the casket. We have only five hours left. It's useless!'

'How can we tell her if she isn't here to tell?' Their uncle looked miserable. 'What a terrible business.'

Simon closed the book he had been reading and looked up. 'We could try to contact the Knights again. If they're Lords of Time or whatever it was Mrs C. called them, they might be able to help us.'

With a sigh, Mrs Frazer gathered up her knitting and followed him into the study. Malcolm and Uncle Henry, leaving Joss asleep on the drawing-room hearthrug in front of the fire, joined them. As before, they sat round the table, and Malcolm placed the key at its centre.

'Shall I put some music on?' The others nodded.

The lights were dimmed as the first sonorous chords of Bach's unaccompanied cello suites rang through the room. For a few minutes nothing happened, then, very faintly at first, the key began to glow. The throbbing bass chord of the violincello seemed to fade, to dissolve into that powerhouse hum they had heard before. It increased in volume until they were caught up, as if in a vortex, spun, whirled in a spiral current, up, up, up, as the light grew brighter and more intense. Then, quite abruptly, everything steadied.

The two boys stood again in the vast, circular vaulted chamber. Around the table sat the company of Knights. This time they were in full armour. In the most central position, as before, sat the man the children called the Knight-King. He, too, was armoured; around his helmet, its visor lifted, shone the golden circlet. His face was grave, yet when he saw them he smiled. They stepped forward and noticed for the first time that two strange children stood beside them — a boy with a pale face and sandy hair, dressed in an old-fashioned Norfolk suit with knickerbockers, and a hard, stiff collar; and a girl in a dark, caped coat, her long red hair tied back under a pink Tam o' Shanter.

'What is it that you wish to ask? Speak — do not be afraid.'

Malcolm cleared his throat nervously.

'It's about the casket. We wanted to ask . . . we wondered . . .'

'You wanted to ask that the casket should be given now to the Captain, and his Forces of the Shadow, in exchange for the life of your friend Bina Henderson. My children, you do not understand what it is you are asking!'

There was a pause.

'It may help you if you are shown something of the history of the casket and its precious contents. Watch!'

The great wall at the back of the chamber now seemed to dissolve into a blank space in which mist swirled.

The Knights had vanished, the four children stood alone.

The girl in the pink tammy spoke. 'This is perfectly ridiculous, Harry! I'm not stopping another moment! They'll be wondering at home what has happened to us.'

'Wait, Lu, wait,' begged the sandy-haired boy. Simon noticed that the two of them took no notice of Malcolm and himself, it was almost as though they were invisible.

The light around them was dimming, but on the huge screen in front of them a vivid picture was forming. It was like watching a film in Cinemascope, but instead of the flatness and distortion one would experience on a cinema screen, the picture was three-dimensional and appeared to surround them. Yet they knew that if they put out their hands to touch they would feel nothing.

A voice spoke. 'You are in the Temple of Poseidon, in ancient Atlantis.'

They saw a broad flight of steps leading to an immense doorway. This they entered and passed along an avenue lined with burnished golden statues, each with an animal's head. They came to some more doors, golden and set with what appeared to be precious stones, but these were barred against them. However, they seemed to pass upwards into a small room under what could only be the great dome of the temple itself. It was completely circular. Round the walls were curtains made of some strange material, almost as if they were composed of vibrating, shifting light which constantly changed colour. As they watched, the colour changed to a deep, almost violet blue. They parted, and through them came the figure of a woman dressed in a plain white robe. They recognised her immediately. It was Mrs Clarke.

In the centre of the room, on a small pillar, stood the casket. The priestess, for that was what they felt her to be, approached, opened it and took from it the small globe of translucent material it contained. She raised it in her hands above her head, and from it streams of light were directed upwards. The dome became transparent. They could see at its apex a shining, multi-faceted crystal. The rays were caught by the crystal and directed downwards over the city below, over the fields, over the ocean; charging everything it touched with its beneficent power.

Yet the scene darkened. A black-coated figure entered the room, lifted the casket. It was taken from the temple. The crystal was shattered. Now they saw the substance being used in underground laboratories, where the androids it had created came marching in rows out of the furnaces to take their places as soldiers, as work forces. Still deadlier things were created, monsters so terrible that they shut their eyes and could not look. Lurid colours gathered above the devastated land. Inhuman, uncaring, the robot armies marched, trampling everything to destruction beneath their feet. The black-robed priests smiled in the temple, while the people wept. Now the clouds grew even darker, the flash of erupting volcanoes split the purple sky. Huge waves rolled, threatening the city. Taller and taller rose the glistening water, until in a last terrific crescendo it crashed over the island, destroying the temple, sweeping away the buildings and the people, drowning Atlantis beneath the sea for ever. The screen darkened completely.

The voice spoke again. 'Atlantis was destroyed, but the casket was saved. It was taken first to Ancient Egypt, then to the Himalayas. The guardian priestess, your friend, carried it on its long journey, facing many hazards. She risked her life — even died, as you know it — several times to protect it. In Peru, with the Incas, later in Spain under the Inquisition. At last she was given the chance of never returning to the earth again, but going to a just reward on a more enlightened planet. Yet, knowing of the growing danger threatening your world, she refused. We come now to the late eighteenth century. The casket had been brought out of hiding to avert a catastrophe. It stayed hidden with the old shop-keeper, Demosthenes, in Edinburgh. He was one of our trusted servants. He knew he was in great peril, and being unable to deliver it in person to the lady he knew as Mistress Clarke, he contacted us and was told that messengers from the future would be sent, and it was to them that he must entrust it. So it was to you, Harry and Lucy, children with unprejudiced minds, that the casket was given. The old man died for his troubles. The rest you know.'

They began, dimly, to perceive the speaker. It was the Knight-King. He stood, half concealed, his cloak wrapped around him.

Harry spoke: 'So, she hasn't died since — not really?'

There was silence, as always when they asked a question they themselves could have answered.

138

'Have you come to a decision?' the Knight-King asked.

Simon stepped forward. 'Is there no alternative? No other way?'

'What do you yourselves suggest?'

'Well, we were wondering if we could — sort of sneak on to the *Nostradamus* — with your help of course — and find the shepherdess and take her away.'

There was a murmur of protest from the girl in the pink tammy.

The Knight-King unloosed his cloak and turned so they could see his face. 'We hoped you might want to do this. But you would have to accomplish it on your own. We would be watching over you, and come to your aid if necessary. But the most important part must be done by yourselves. And you have less than three hours.'

Simon and Malcolm spoke almost together.

'What must we do?'

'That is what you must decide. As I have explained, we can help you and watch over you, but you must make your own plans.'

'Could we make a false shepherdess and substitute it for the one Bina's imprisoned in,' Malcolm suggested to his cousin.

'How?' Simon replied. 'We just haven't got enough time.'

Harry was talking to his sister. 'If only we had some of the substance perhaps we could make a shepherdess from it . . .'

The Knight-King spoke. 'We can provide you with a little of the substance, enough to serve your purpose.'

'Thank you — but how in heaven's name are we to make a shepherdess when we haven't got a copy — not even a photograph!' Malcolm sounded despairing.

'And there's so little *time* . . .'

Things were fading. A voice spoke and this time it was Mrs Clarke.

'Nothing in the memory is permanently lost. Don't be so lazy. If you try you will have total recall.' Total recall, total recall, the walls echoed, and the humming began again. They plunged downwards into darkness, in which a clock was ticking. It struck ten.

The darkness cleared and they were in Uncle Henry's study.

Or were they? For it had altered in a peculiar way. There was a dark red flock wallpaper on the walls, there were brackets with gaslights popping in them behind pink glass shades. A bright coal fire burned in the grate, and the round central table was covered with an ink-stained chenille cloth.

In the centre of the table was a white crochet mat, and on it swayed a small sphere, like an iridescent bubble.

The two strange children were sitting on the other side of the table. The girl, Lucy, had taken off her coat and beret and was glaring at them. 'I don't know what they are doing here,' she said to her brother. 'They've no business to be here. I don't know what Mother will say.'

Simon saw how difficult it would be to explain to her.

'Listen,' he said. 'We're here to help, we haven't got time for explanations. We must concentrate on making the china shepherdess, and you have to show us how. After all, you were the one who used to make things.'

Lucy blushed red and looked stubborn.

'Come now, Lucy,' ordered Mrs Clarke's voice from somewhere near the ceiling. 'You have an important part to play, remember. It was owing to you that the box was opened and all the trouble started. You learned how to manipulate the etheric substance, and now you have been sent back to childhood to do it again — to make amends . . .'

The voice was so faint that they could not be sure they had heard the final words correctly.

'Mrs Clarke!' squeaked Henry, whose voice was breaking.

No answer.

'We're on our own now,' Simon told them, 'and we have to work fast. Build up a picture in your mind.'

'But she never saw the shepherdess,' Malcolm objected. 'We'll have to show her.'

'Tell me,' Lucy ordered. She had shut her eyes. Her voice was more like their grandmother's. 'Look — I'm moulding it now.'

They looked. A triangle, a wobbly blancmange, five inches high. White, no colour, amorphous, opaque.

'The head,' commanded Lucy. 'Concentrate on the head!'

'A silly, simpering face,' Simon told her. 'Under a flat hat, with ribbons. Yellow curls.'

The head began to appear, a little on one side. Lucy straightened it. She made the neck. 'What colour of dress?' she enquired.

'Green, wasn't it?' Malcolm asked tentatively. Lucy stretched out her hand. Power seemed to flow from her fingers into his. He saw more distinctly, in three dimensions. 'A dark red overdress,' he said quietly. 'And a white petticoat under it, sprigged with little pink flowers.'

'Don't forget the bright green grass and the lamb at her feet,' put in Simon.

'From the picture you're giving me, I see something behind her,' Lucy said. 'What is it? A wall?'

'No,' Simon said firmly. He had taken her other hand. 'I know what it was. A tree. A sort of stunted tree.'

Amongst argument, the figure was fashioned. Harry was left out. He sat dejected, arms folded.

'Oh, it's wobbling again. We must make it solid.'

Slowly, the shepherdess turned on the mat.

'It's a bit woolly here, isn't it? That's better. Now, turn it round again. Something's missing. Oh, yes, I know — a bunch of flowers, in her lap.'

Harry spoke. 'What about putting in some fine cracks all over? After all, it's nearly two hundred and fifty years old.'

'It wouldn't be two hundred and fifty years old if it's on the *Nostradamus* in 1798, stupid!' There was some argument, but at last it was agreed that the figure, having been brought back from the twentieth century, would look as it had appeared in the museum. A fine network of hairline cracks in the glaze was added. The clock struck the half hour.

'It's done,' Simon sighed. 'For better or worse. Leave off concentrating. Let's seal it.'

'How do you suggest we do that, Mr Know-all?'

'Be quiet, Lu,' ordered Harry. 'Let's all hold our hands over it. I'm sure we're being helped.'

They stood, their arms outstretched, the tips of their fingers touching.

'My fingers tingle!'

'So do mine!'

'And mine!'

They let their hands drop. A minute's pause, then, 'Touch it gently,' Simon told them.

Lucy put out her hand and with one finger carefully touched the little china figurine. Then, without a word, she picked it up and passed it round. It shone, it was smooth and solid. As far as they could judge it was a perfect copy.

'Now what? The ship?'

'Oh yes,' Lucy said scornfully, 'you boys would start off at once without thinking of what would happen if it got broken. Here, put it in this!'

She took up a little pink satin bag with a draw-string at the neck, shook out some reels of cotton, a needlecase and a pair of scissors and, showing them it had a padded lining, placed the shepherdess within. She drew the cords tight.

Malcolm placed it carefully in the pocket of his anorak.

'The key,' Simon said. 'Have you got the key?'

'Yes, it's round my neck.'

'Take care of it, whatever you do,' begged Harry.

'How on earth do we get there — to the *Nostradamus*?'

'That's Harry's business,' said Lucy primly, putting on her coat and adjusting her tam o' shanter. 'He was the one who *sent* the ball to places. That was what he was good at. Now he must concentrate and send the shepherdess *and* us to the ship. Hold hands! Now, Harry, *think*,'

'Oh, Lu, I don't believe I can . . .'

'Ha-rry!'

Malcolm took Simon's hand, who took Harry's, who took Lucy's, who took Malcolm's.

Now the circle was complete.

It was a circle of power.

The humming began again, and as it did so the table, the study, the crackling fire all melted away.

CHAPTER SEVENTEEN

Light came to them gradually. They were out of doors on a cold, wet night, with a stinging salt wind. Under their feet were cobblestones, and on their right the masts of ships, their dark bulks swinging at anchor at a quay side.

On their left was a wide square, bordered by tall, leering houses with crow-stepped gables.

Figures moved on one of the ships, a man with a lantern, giving orders. From a waggon, sacks were loaded up a gangplank. Up aloft, men worked in the rigging.

The four children stood watching.

Then the red-haired girl spoke. 'Well, Harry, if we have to go aboard the Captain's ship, like your Mrs Clarke said —'

'It wasn't Mrs Clarke,' interrupted Malcolm; but the girl took as much notice as if he had not spoken.

'— as Mrs Clarke said,' she continued. 'Then you'd best waste no more time. It's no use catching our death by hanging around in this horrid place!'

The sandy boy spoke in a squeaky, breaking voice: 'That's all very well, Lu, but which is the *Nostradamus*? And, even if we did know, how the dickens could we get aboard without being seen?'

Simon crossed over to the other two. 'Listen —' he started, but Lucy interrupted him. 'Who *are* you? I asked you before, and you never answered!'

'Look, it's not important, just say we're friends who have been

144

sent to help. We have to stick together. That's Malcolm, and I'm Simon.'

'There's something familiar about you two,' Harry said, his voice puzzled. 'You must be — someone I know, but you're dressed so oddly —'

'We're relations of yours, really,' Malcolm began to explain in spite of Simon's attempts to silence him. 'Out of the future, you know. We're — well, *she's* our grandmother!'

He indicated Lucy, who stood glaring at him. 'The *cat's* grandmother! I've never heard such nonsense in all my life. Don't trust them, Harry, this is some trick of the Captain's. Ignore them!'

'Show them the key, Mal,' Simon ordered.

Malcolm pulled out the key and held it up.

'The key!' cried Harry. 'Look, Lu — they've got the key, and I thought I had it safe in my drawer at home! Who are you really? Did Mrs Clarke send you?'

'Yes, in a way she did. But we're wasting time. We must find and board the ship, that's the important part.'

They crept close to the quay, hiding in the long shadows. Peering into the gloom they tried to make out the ships' names.

'Not that one,' Malcolm said, pointing to the three-masted schooner which they had earlier watched loading. 'She's British — the *Lady Jayne* something from Newhaven.'

'And not this one,' Simon said, peering at a ketch that lay alongside. 'I can't make the name out, but she comes from Aberdeen, and anyway, the *Nostradamus* was a much bigger ship, an old man-of-war.'

They passed two more ships, then Harry uttered a faint cry.

'This one! This is it, I'm sure this is it!'

They stopped, looking at the bulk towering above them. It was in total darkness. Unlike the other boats; no life, no movement disturbed the deck, no light glimmered.

'It's just a hulk,' said Lucy. 'It looks as if it had been abandoned.'

Simon pointed. High up on the stern, in the faint glow of

the lantern which hung from the prow of a neighbouring schooner, they made out the words "NOSTRA DAMUS — AMSTERDAM".

Before them was a rickety gangplank with no supports.

Lucy stifled a scream with her gloved hand.

'A rat — look, going up the gangway!'

'Single file,' breathed Simon.

'He's sure to be up there. He'll spot us.' Harry sounded apprehensive.

'I'll go first,' Malcolm said bravely.

'No, you've got the key. You should go last, to guard our rear. I'll go first, then Harry, then Lucy, and then you,' Simon decided.

He stepped onto the slimy, rotting plank. On hands and knees he crawled up. Harry followed, shaking and slithering; then Lucy, surprisingly fast, but making little moans of disgust under her breath; and last, Malcolm, as if he did it every day. One by one they dropped cautiously down onto the deck. They listened. Timbers creaked in the shore-wind's whine; that was all. There was an eerie feeling of being watched.

'Where do we go now?' Harry shivered miserably, pulling his coat collar up. Malcolm was slowly exploring the deck. Moment by moment there was the sense of the ship coming to slow, menacing life beneath them, like some saurian reptile waking from a long hibernation.

'Where's he disappeared to *now*?' Lucy said irritably. She was covering up her fear better than her brother, although her teeth were chattering with the cold. 'I thought we were supposed to stick together.'

Malcolm's footsteps returned. He sounded excited. 'There are cannon on deck, and they look as though they're in working order.'

'Well, obviously there are, you stupid boy. It's a captured warship. Even I know that,' Lucy said sharply. 'But now you've got us here, what are we going to do now? Shouldn't we be looking for the Captain's cabin? If he's got anything hidden, it's most likely to be there.'

In the faint light from a drunken, lopsided moon which now split the rain clouds, they walked forward. In front of them, on deck level, was a door. They tried it. It was unlocked; opening stiffly, creaking on rusty hinges, it swung back and they entered. They looked around. They were in a large cabin, full of heavy dark furniture. Moonlight streamed through the leaded glass windows which looked onto the deck. Indeed, it seemed to them that the cabin had some radiance of its own, some sort of eerie, pallid phosphorescence. A slight rocking movement of the ship sent, from minute to minute, the striped reflection of harbour lights across the interior.

On the table a book lay open, a quill pen beside the page.

Malcolm produced a pencil torch from the pocket of his anorak. By its light they read:

January 8th, 1798. This day, at the close of the third watch, was James Taggart, known as Demosthenes, sent back to his Maker. May this be a lesson to all Meddlers.

'Poor old Demosthenes, what a rotten shame.'

'Stop that, Harry!' ordered his sister. 'Look *here*!'

In the centre of the page, the ink hardly dry on the paper, was written:

To be so dealt with:
  Alison Lucy Gilchrist
  Henry Charles Gilchrist
  Malcolm Gordon Short
  Simon Waldersley

The signature below was illegible.

'Those are our names!'

'What are they doing here?'

'I shall faint, I know I shall!'

'Shut up,' ordered Malcolm. 'Look! The cabinet! Over in that corner — *that's* what we ought to be thinking about.' They hurried over. Fixed high in the corner of the room was a cupboard, its leaded panes grimy with dust.

Malcolm shone his torch. There, on a shelf, behind the dirty glass was the shepherdess. He tried the door but it was locked.

'The key,' Simon said excitedly. 'Hold up the key!'

Malcolm held the key over the lock. The door swung open easily.

'Bina, we're here,' he breathed. 'Hang on, we've come to —'

'Someone's coming!' Simon's voice was strained. 'Quick, change them over.' Malcolm took the bag from his pocket. He reached into it, took out the false shepherdess and placed it on the shelf. Then, with infinite care, he took the real one, placed her in the bag, and returned the bag to his pocket. Holding up the key he closed the door and heard the key turn in the lock. As he swung round, the light in his torch dimmed down to a red filament; at the same moment the moon slunk behind a cloud. They were plunged into darkness. Simon, who was nearest the cabin door, grabbed the handle and tried to open it. It was locked fast.

The children panicked, beating upon the door. In their terror they forgot everything, the key, the Light, the Knights, Mrs Clarke, forgot even Bina-inside-the-shepherdess. Their thoughts were on one thing and one thing only — to escape alive and unhurt. It was like an unheard scream inside them. But there was worse horror to come. They became aware that the cabin was filled with another sound, a blattering downbeat, a surge, a sway, a sickening stench. Leathery wings brushed their faces, their hair.

'Bats!' shouted Harry. 'Hundreds of them. Guard your throats!'

Lucy shrieked. 'Oh, I'm bitten! On the thumb! It's bleeding like anything! Keep off! Keep them away from me! Help! Help! Help!'

And now they heard, or thought they heard — was it the wind rising? Or was it a laugh? A triumphant, diabolical laugh. Again it sounded, more distinctly, and at that moment Simon suddenly came to himself. 'Stop it,' he shouted. 'Stop it, all of you! Malcolm, remember the key! Keep close to him you others, and for heaven's sake, keep still. Have you got it, Mal?'

Fending off the bats with one hand, Malcolm scrabbled round

his neck with the other; at last his fingers clasped over its metallic coldness.

'Lucy, Harry,' he could hear his cousin calling. His voice seemed to get fainter. In the distance Lucy's sobs seemed to diminish, once he thought he heard Harry shout. He held up the key and it began, almost immediately, to glow. White, piercing rays sprang from it, flowing out in all directions. The bats retreated, they seemed to dissolve, vanish into thin air. The light illuminated the great cabin and showed him to be completely alone. Silence fell. As the glow faded, Malcolm held the key, pressing it to his chest for comfort. 'Si!' he shouted. 'Harry! Lucy! Where have you gone?'

There was no answer.

Emptiness and almost complete darkness filled the cabin — no moon, no harbour lights, and the torch was still not working. He felt stifled in the airless gloom. Feeling his way over to the wall, he sat down on the floor, his back against it. It was then that he first became aware of the movement of the ship. Not the gentle rocking which they had felt when they boarded it in the harbour, but a steady rise and fall; a shuddering and a creaking of timbers as the old vessel braced itself against the waves. There was a sharp crack from somewhere above his head. Malcolm started violently — then recognised the sound. It was not a pistol shot, but the sound of a canvas sail flapping as the wind filled it. They were at sea. There was a small window with thickly leaded panes above his head. Climbing on a bench, he managed to force the catch and open it. A great gust of salt air revived him. Very far away, it seemed to him, the lights of the harbour receded.

He sank down onto the bench and, as he did so, heard a thundering of feet on the deck above him. Almost immediately, the cabin door burst open. There was no time to hide — and nowhere to go. Two men entered; he could not see their faces. One of them grabbed him, pinioning his arms behind him. He smelt sweat and the pungent aroma of tobacco. Without speaking, they pulled him roughly to his feet and manhandled him out of the cabin. He could not quite convince himself that it wasn't a nightmare, that at any moment he would wake in his nice warm bed at home — but the men felt real enough.

One of them covered his head with a piece of sacking, smelling strongly of rotten fish. Then he felt himself half-dragged, half-pushed, over the wooden boards of the deck and hurled into what felt like empty space. He expected to feel the splash of water and braced himself, but instead hit something yielding and slippery, which broke his fall. As he landed, his hand, which he had spread out in front of him, dragged on the key cord and he felt it snap. The key plummeted from his neck. One moment he was clutching it — the next his fingers had spread out to check his fall — a tug, a snap, and it was lost. For a moment he lay stunned. Then, gradually, he was aware of voices.

'I tell you, my leg's broken. It's all your Mistress Clarke's fault. She got us into this and now she's deserted us. And how do you propose to get us out, Harry, tell me that!'

Malcolm sat up. The blindfold had fallen off as he fell, and he could dimly make out that he was sitting on a pile of sailcloth or tarpaulin, spread over what felt like bales of hay. He was obviously in the hold. It was pitch black except for a faint light seeping from cracks round an oblong shape in the ceiling — presumably the trapdoor through which he had been thrown.

'Lucy — Harry!' he called softly. 'Simon — are you there?'

Lucy's voice continued undisturbed, as though he had not spoken.

'Well, Harry, did you hear me? I think I'm going to be sick!'

'You're jolly well *not* going to be sick,' Harry's voice grumbled from somewhere on Malcolm's left. 'Anyway, your leg isn't broken. When Waterson broke his leg in the school match he fainted clean away, and —'

'Harry, for heaven's sake, can't you hear me?' Malcolm called desperately.

'How d'you know I didn't faint? I did, so there! You know nothing about it. I wish I were home with Mouncie. Fff — the pain! It's agony, you just have no idea. We'll never get out of here alive, and it's all your fault, you and your precious Mrs Clarke!'

'Are you two doing this on purpose?' Malcolm demanded. 'If so, it's not funny.' He suddenly remembered the little china shepherdess and with a stab of fear felt in his pocket. Miraculously, she seemed to have survived unbroken. 'We've got to find the key,' he continued. 'It came off the cord when I fell down just now. If you both help we might be able to locate it. Feel around very carefully with your hands on the floor.'

'It's got nothing to do with Mrs Clarke. It was all your fault to start off with, because you opened the casket . . .' Harry's squeaky voice seemed to be growing fainter. Soon, although Malcolm could still hear their grumbling, he could no longer distinguish the words. He called Simon's name, but there was no answer. And then again he heard, coming from a point directly overhead, that peal of devilish laughter.

He looked up and saw that the trapdoor had been removed. Outlined blackly against the paler dark of the night sky, he saw the familiar silhouette, the broad-brimmed hat, the face a white blur. Only the eyes, deep in their cavernous sockets, seemed to glow; little pinpoints of red. He was conscious of a sibilant whisper close to his ear.

'No use trying any more, is it? Might as well give in. Time is so short, almost over, and the odds against finding the key are too great. The others have all given up already, you know that. So, Malcolm, unless you surrender there's very little chance of getting out of here alive, is there? *And you know what I want from you.*'

Yes, thought Malcolm, feeling with his hand the small bag in his pocket, I know. But now no saving voice with consoling, strengthening message came to him, such as had saved them in the old crumbling house. There were no directions as to where the key was to be found. He was truly on his own. And yet, was he?

There came to him, there in the darkness, the absolute certainty that the power, whatever it was, lay within him. The key was just a symbol. He began concentrating his mind, trying to visualise the Light as they had done with Bina. He saw it like a white searchlight, burning down through the night into the darkness of the hold. When he opened his eyes the Captain had disappeared and an incandescent glow which seemed to have no visible source lit the blackness and showed him Simon, lying inert on the floor some distance from him. At his feet, gleaming palely, was the key.

'Simon! Are you hurt?'

'I don't think so — my back aches a bit when I move. What happened?'

'We were thrown into the hold. Where are the others?'

'I don't know, I think I was knocked unconscious. Anyway they're not here now. Mal, what's that light? It's not the key, is it?'

'No — I can't explain now, tell you later. The important thing is that I've still got the shepherdess safe. If only we could figure out a way to . . .' He stopped. Simon was staring up and beyond him, a look of horror on his face. Malcolm turned, knowing what he would see. The light in the hold dimmed slowly as the white face peered down upon them once more. He held something out to them, his black-gloved hand a claw. As the fingers slowly opened, fragments of china fell from them; a silly, simpering head, the trunk of a tree, a lamb. They shattered on the boards.

'Such *clever* boys,' the voice hissed above them. 'And such a waste of precious material. However, I dare say I will find a way to — reconstitute it. And now, if you please, I would like my property returned.' Something clicked, the long barrel of a pistol pointed at them. Behind him they dimly made out other heads, other eyes glowing. They clutched each other.

Malcolm felt for the key, held it. As he did so, the light around them seemed to swell. He felt strangely unafraid. The faces round the trapdoor fell back and they seemed to rise, still holding onto one another, through the opening and up above the deck. There was a low humming sound as if from some unimaginably powerful dynamo.

As they looked down on the ship there came a sharp roll of

thunder and a flash of lightning, which illuminated the vessel from mast to stern.

'Look — look over there,' Malcolm pointed.

Down a great ribbon of light, which seemed to stretch like a road before them, came the Knights, their armour gleaming, their banners waving with the red encircled cross. At their head rode two figures, one with a purple cloak, a golden crown around his head, the other unarmed, swathed in a blue mantle, her red-gold hair an aureole around her.

There came the great crash and boom of cannons. They looked down again. On the rear mast deck of his ship stood the Captain. He seemed to have swollen, grown monstrous. Behind him, rising from the depths, came the dark armies, their black armour gleaming dully, their great bat wings unfurling.

Again the cannon boomed. The air was filled with a great cloud of smoke, within which red fire burned. When it cleared the Knights still advanced, their leaders unscathed. A magnesium flare of lightning illuminated the scene as they swept to the attack. As it crackled over the black hordes they seemed to shrink, to fall back. There was another boom from the guns and a thick pall of black smoke arose, hiding the battle from the watchers.

As it cleared, the boys could make out that the ship was listing badly. The humming sound had increased and, as if they had become aware of it, the dark armies were retreating, dissolving into mist. A trumpet call, thin and silvery, pierced the air and, on an instant, the ranks of the Knights wheeled, banner still proudly flying, and rode back into the clouds. On the deck of the ship, which was sinking ever lower into the water, stood three figures.

The Captain dwindled, he lost height, he was bowed down.

'Why don't they finish him off now?' cried Malcolm. 'Why don't they —'

'Look, Mal, look!'

The Captain, his hands over his face to shield him from the light, was turning, doubling, running into ever-increasing darkness. A beam of light followed him. As it touched him he let

153

out a terrible scream of agony and fell forward. One hand crept out.

The Knight-King spoke.

'You wish to undo what has been done?'

'If I must — yes, yes.'

'Release the girl, Robina Henderson. Let her go freely. This is your first step on a long pilgrimage.'

'The casket, then! The casket! I must have the casket!'

'You have no more power to bargain with — surely you realise that.'

There was silence for an instant, then again the scream.

'I am burning. Save me!'

'You yourself cause the burning, no other.'

'What must I do?'

'Release the child of your own free will!'

'Never, never! With her goes all power, with her goes the casket and its contents! In a few minutes the substance will be unsealed — and all my striving would be gone for nothing!'

The darkness around him was now lit by a thousand flickering darting scarlet arrows of rage, hatred and resentment, which, before their eyes, became small, licking tongues of flame.

The Captain screamed once more. 'I burn! I shall perish!'

'You are being consumed by the flames of your own passion. Once you possessed what you desire you would burn the world,' came the Knight-King's calm voice. 'In burning the world, you yourself would be consumed, for evil destroys itself. Only you can quench these flames.'

The Captain writhed, rolling in agony on the ground.

'Must I give up — everything?'

'Yes, to gain everything.'

At last, the voice, dry as sticks crackling, spoke for the last time, with great difficulty.

'I release the child Robina Henderson — from my power — now and henceforth — forever —'

The flames died. The light faded. Darkness enveloped the scene.

Suddenly, a new voice spoke beside the boys.

It was Bina.

'Simon! Is that you Simon? Malcolm? Where are you?'

'Bina! Are you OK? We're on the *Nostradamus* — at least, we were. There's been a most terrific battle and —'

'It's all over, the Captain's surrendered all power over to the Knight-King and Mrs Clarke, and —'

Bina's voice cut in, joyfully. 'I can *see*, Malcolm! I'm in a little room, in bed — I think it's a hospital, yes, a nurse is just coming in —'

Abruptly, the contact was broken. Malcolm felt in the little bag. empty. The china shepherdess was gone. At that moment the light came back and they heard the humming once more. It grew and grew, vibrating around them like a great spinning top. They seemed to be moving; closing their eyes against the blinding whiteness of the light, they had the sensation of being sucked through space. They lost consciousness. When they opened their eyes again, they were lying on the floor of their uncle's study, and he and Mrs Frazer were bending anxiously over them.

CHAPTER EIGHTEEN

It was a week later.

Simon and Malcolm had come to say goodbye to Bina, who was allowed home to finish her convalescence. She was still in bed, but more her old self.

'So it's back to school for you two,' she said.

'The day after tomorrow for me,' Malcolm said, 'and next week for Si.'

'I'm flying back to New York on Friday. But I'll be back in the Summer for the Festival.'

'That's nice,' she said softly. She was still pale, but had lost most of her bandages. 'Your uncle will miss you. And all the excitement,' she added. 'Still, I expect he'll be seeing a bit more of your grannie in the future.'

She handed the boys a fruit dish. 'I can't stand grapes,' she told them. 'I'm sick of them, eat the lot.' She leaned languidly back against her pillows. 'Well, come on, entertain me. I want to know the last chapter of the story. No, not the heavenly visit — I find that boring and unbelievable, but you haven't told me what happened after you woke up to find yourself back at Linlithgow Avenue.'

'Uncle and Gran were bending over us, looking scared out of their minds,' Malcolm told her. 'Gran had a glass of water in her hand and kept telling us to drink it. I've never seen her so agitated.'

Simon spat a grape pip out into his hand and looked for

somewhere to put it. 'You could see they felt terrifically guilty — they must have thought we were never going to wake from our coma.' He stole a glance at Bina as he said this, but she only handed him a saucer from the bedside table, saying, 'Put it in there, for heaven's sake! So what did they say?'

'Oh, the usual things — did we feel all right, etc., etc. *You* know.'

'We kept telling them we were OK, but Gran obviously didn't believe us. So in the end we told them the whole story.'

'And?'

'They didn't really seem to take it in. Gran said she remembered nothing about it. Uncle H said he had a hazy recollection of being on board a ship, and being frightened, and falling. He kept saying "We held you in the light, you know, every second after we woke up."' Simon smiled at the recollection.

'So they admitted they'd been off and away?' Bina enquired.

'*She* didn't,' Malcolm told her. 'She said she'd been unconscious every minute of the time, and scared silly because we were all out for the count.'

'Anyway, I'll tell you something interesting,' Simon said, reaching for another grape. 'You remember we told you that Mal heard her complaining that she'd broken her leg when we were thrown into the hold of the Nostradamus? And that she'd been bitten by a bat? Well, she's complaining of a very sore ankle, and she has a cut on her thumb covered in a plaster! When we asked her about it she said she had no idea how it had come there.'

'She must have looked very sweet in her pink tammy,' Bina said. 'I wish I could have seem them both.'

'And there's one last inexplicable thing more, isn't there, Mal? Tell her about the letter.'

'OK, then we must go. We've been here nearly an hour and your mother told us we mustn't overexcite you—'

'What rubbish!' cut in Bina.

'— anyway, the day before yesterday, Uncle Henry received a letter. He'd been very down in the dumps since it all happened,

157

felt he'd failed, not been of any use, you can imagine the sort of thing. And then this letter arrived. In a long, pale-grey envelope, smelling of violets, addressed to him in a sloping hand —'

'In violet ink, I suppose,' Bina said, sniffing.

'If you don't keep quiet I won't finish the story. Well, first of all he took it into his study and closed the door. He was there for ages — nearly an hour. Then he came out, and you should have seen his face! He was smiling all over. He showed us the letter, let us read it.'

'What did it *say*? I suppose it was from her, Mrs C?'

'Oh yes. It began "My dear old friend, dear Harry." Then it went on to say that he was not to think he'd failed this time, because his support in the background had made it possible for us to do what we had to do, and without him we couldn't have done it, and how grateful she was to him and us. What came next, Si?'

'She said,' Simon frowned, trying to see the pages in his mind's eye, 'that the substance had been resealed in the casket, and that it was going into the safest keeping ever, until the day man had learned sufficient humility and brotherly love to make the right use of it, and she hoped that day was not too far off, but that a great deal remained to be done. Then there was something about how a great many battles were still to be fought, and we must hold the whole world in the Force Field of the Light continually, as our help was desperately needed by the Knights and herself, and by those above them.'

'And what about the Captain — did she mention him?'

'Yes,' said Malcolm. 'She said something about us being disappointed because they did not kill him when they had the chance, but we were to understand that — what was the phrase she used? — something about a furnace.'

'That he will come out of the furnace bright and burnished,' quoted Simon. 'And then she said that although we would not see her again in this lifetime, she would be watching over us, so she signed herself with love, his Lalla — that was the silly secret name he called her.'

'Incredible!' was Bina's comment. 'I'd like to see that letter.'

'Well, you can't — that's the annoying thing about it,' Simon told her regretfully. 'It's disappeared. Right out of a locked drawer in the bureau in Uncle's room, at the same time as the key, which was beside it, and which I'd given back to him. And though we've searched the house, we can't find either of them.'

'They won't be found,' Malcolm decided.

'Of course they won't,' agreed Bina. 'It's finished, all of it. I think I want to forget everything about it as soon as possible.'

'But you can't, Bina,' Malcolm said. 'It happened.'

Bina snuggled down under the coverlets.

'I'm tired. Goodbye! Write to me, both of you. We're all irrevocably joined, isn't that so?' She closed her eyes.

They said goodbye and left the room. On the landing they paused.

'She won't, you know,' Simon reassured Malcolm.

'Won't what?'

'Won't forget,' Simon said. 'None of us can. We've been — like "branded".' He laughed self-consciously. Then he made his face solemn to say goodbye to Mrs Henderson at the foot of the stairs.

They walked out into winter sunshine.

'She talked to me, when you went down to help carry away the tea tray,' Simon said.

'Yes?'

'She saw more than she let on. On board. She saw you taking her out and putting her in the bag. Then, she said the figure just melted. For a moment she was with us, and then she saw him, the Captain, dwindling away.'

'So?'

'Well, she knows we saved her — that's what she meant about being irrevocably joined.'

They shuffled leaves, reluctant to go in.

'Does she realise it all happened because she panicked and ran away?'

'I'm certain she does. She doesn't want to talk about it, that's

159

all. You know Bina. she'll probably never speak of it again, but somewhere deep down inside her, she'll remember.'

'I wonder what happened to the shepherdess?'

'Bet you anything it's back in the museum.' Simon began to run. 'Come on, race you to the end of the road.' Malcolm pounded after him.

'Some day,' he puffed, 'some day I shall go there to find out.'

They stopped, gasping for breath, when they reached the cul-de-sac. A chill wind sprang up about their feet, driving the dead leaves before it. It made the noise of a long skirt rustling over the ground, and both boys, for an instant stopping, sniffing the air, thought they smelt violets in January.